Unravelling Oliver

LIZ NUGENT

PENGUIN

IRELAND

PENGUIN IRELAND

Published by the Penguin Group
Penguin Ireland, 25 St Stephen's Green, Dublin 2, Ireland (a division of Penguin Books Ltd)
Penguin Books Ltd, 80 Strand, London WC2R ORL, England
Penguin Group (USA) Inc., 375 Hudson Street, New York, New York 10014, USA
Penguin Group (Australia), 707 Collins Street, Melbourne, Victoria 3008, Australia
(a division of Pearson Australia Group Pty Ltd)
Penguin Group (Canada), 90 Eglinton Avenue East, Suite 700, Toronto, Ontario, Canada M4P 2Y3
(a division of Pearson Penguin Canada Inc.)
Penguin Books India Pvt Ltd, 11 Community Centre, Panchsheel Park, New Delhi – 110 017, India
Penguin Group (NZ), 67 Apollo Drive, Rosedale, Auckland 0632, New Zealand
(a division of Pearson New Zealand Ltd)
Penguin Books (South Africa) (Pty) Ltd, Block D, Rosebank Office Park,
181 Jan Smuts Avenue, Parktown North, Gauteng 2193, South Africa

Penguin Books Ltd, Registered Offices: 80 Strand, London WC2R ORL, England

www.penguin.com

First published 2014
003

Copyright © Liz Nugent, 2014

The moral right of the author has been asserted

Set in 13.5/16pt Garamond MT Std
Typeset by Jouve (UK), Milton Keynes
Printed in Great Britain by Clays Ltd, St Ives plc

A CIP catalogue record for this book is available from the British Library

ISBN: 978–1–844–88309–7

www.greenpenguin.co.uk

Unravelling Oliver

For my mum, with love and gratitude

1. Oliver

I expected more of a reaction the first time I hit her. She just lay on the floor holding her jaw. Staring at me. Silent. She didn't even seem to be surprised.

I was surprised. I hadn't planned to do it. Usually when you hear about this kind of thing, it is the 1950s, and the husband comes home drunk to his slovenly wife from the pub and finds that his dinner is cold. On the contrary, it was 12 November 2011, a wintry Saturday evening on a south Dublin avenue, and Alice had prepared a delicious meal: lamb tagine, served on a bed of couscous, with pitta bread and a side dish of mint yoghurt. Though the lamb was a tad lukewarm by the time she presented it, I really couldn't fault it. I had washed the meal down with two glasses of Sancerre, while Alice prepared the raspberry roulade for serving. I certainly wasn't drunk.

But now, here she lay; the lower half of her body nearly hidden behind the legs of our mahogany dining table, her arms, head and torso curled inwards like a question mark. How had she fallen into that shape? There must have been considerable force behind my closed fist. If the glass had been in my hand, would I have stopped and put it down before I hit her? Or would I have smashed it into her face? Would it have shattered on contact and torn her pale skin? Could I have scarred her for life? It's very hard to know.

The words that come to mind are 'circumstances beyond our control'. I emphasize the word 'our', because, although I should not have done it, she really should not have provoked me.

The phone rang. Maybe I should have ignored it, but it might have been important.

'Hello?'

'Oliver. It's Moya. How are things?'

These rhetorical questions irritate me. 'How are things?', indeed.

Sorry, Moya, I've just punched Alice in the face and she's lying on the floor. And we've had a marvellous dinner.

Of course, I didn't say that. I made some ham-fisted attempt at an excuse and bade her farewell. I waited for the reciprocal adieu.

There was a moment's silence and then:

'Don't you want to know how I am? Where I am?'

I was short and to the point. 'No.'

Another silence. And then, whispered, 'Oh right, OK, is Alice there?'

Go away, you stupid irritating woman.

I didn't say that either. I told her that now was not a good time. She tried to inveigle me into a conversation, prattling about her new life in France. Even amid the turmoil, I could tell that she wanted me to be jealous. Bloody Moya. I ended the conversation politely but firmly.

I thought that the decent thing to do was for me to leave the house immediately. Not permanently, you understand. I thought there was more chance of Alice getting up off the floor if I wasn't looming over her. I went to get my coat from its peg in the hall. It was a little difficult to do up the buttons. My hands suddenly seemed to be too large for my gloves.

Two hours later, I was on my third brandy in Nash's. Nervously, I buttoned and unbuttoned my shirt cuffs. It is a habit from childhood, a thing I do when I am distressed. Even John-Joe commented on my rattled demeanour when he served me. Brandy would not have been my normal tipple. But I had had a shock, you see. Now I *was* drunk.

I wanted to phone Alice to see if she was all right, but I had left my mobile behind and I thought that perhaps borrowing somebody's phone would make a bigger deal of the situation than it warranted. Don't get me wrong, I knew it was serious. A significant error of judgement had been made. She should not have ended up on the floor.

I am aware that I am not the easiest of people. Alice has told me so. I have no friends, for example. I used to, many years ago, but that really didn't work out. We drifted apart and I let them go – voluntarily, I suppose. Friends are just people who remind you of your failings. I have several acquaintances. I have no family either to speak of. Not in the sense that matters.

Over the years, Alice has never pried, has never been too curious. In fact, I would describe her as habitually obedient with just an occasional rebellion. I am not, have never been, violent.

I went to the bar and bought a packet of cigarettes. Strong ones. I was worried that my hands were still unsteady. Isn't brandy supposed to help at a time like this? Or is that an old wives' tale? Old wives.

Outside in the 'beer garden' (a yard with half a roof beside the front door), I lit my first cigarette in years. Barney Dwyer, a neighbour from the Villas, approached from the public bar. Barney spent more time in the beer garden than inside the pub.

'Thought you were off them?' he said.

'I am.'

'Jaysus,' said he, a swagger in his voice and sucking on a Rothmans, 'they couldn't break me.'

Here we go. Barney prided himself on his forty-a-day habit. When the smoking ban was introduced, most of us did our best to quit. I am proud to say that I was the first to succeed. I became known as the man with a 'will of iron'. Barney, on the other hand, made no such attempt. If Barney had never smoked, he would have started the day the ban was introduced. A contrary bugger if ever there was one. Thin head, big ears.

'Welcome back,' he said.

'I'm not *back*, I'm just having the one. It's been a bad day.'

'Jaysus, Oliver, it's never just the one. You're back on the fags. Face it.'

I threw my almost smoked cigarette on the ground. Stamped on it. Tossed the packet containing nineteen cigarettes at Barney.

'Keep them,' I said. 'Go on, kill yourself.'

My wife had finally brought out the worst in me. It was most unexpected. I had always been fond of her, in my way. She was a marvellous cook, for example, after all the gourmet cuisine courses I made sure she attended. Also, she could be very athletic in bed, which was nice. It is

4

terribly sad to think of such things now, considering her current state.

We met at the launch of a book she had illustrated back in 1982. My agent wanted me to meet her with a view to her doing the illustrations for a children's book I had written that he was pushing around to publishers. I resisted the idea of illustrations initially. They would just distract from my text, I thought, but my agent, I admit it, was right. The drawings made my books far more marketable. We were introduced and I like to think there was an immediate . . . something. Spark is not the right word, but an acknowledgement of sorts. Some people call that love at first sight. I am not so naïve.

Neither of us was in the first flush of youth. Both in our late twenties, I think. But she was lovely in a soft way. I liked her quietness and she made few or no demands on me. She just accepted whatever attention I gave her, and then withdrew into the background without complaint when I did not require her presence.

The wedding happened very quickly. There was nothing to be gained by hanging about. Her frail mother and half-witted brother stood behind us at the altar. No family on my side, of course. We didn't bother with the palaver of a hotel reception. We had a rowdy meal in a city-centre bistro owned by a former college friend, Michael. Barney was there. Back then I quite liked him. He was very emotional at the wedding, more than anybody else. One couldn't blame him, I suppose.

We rented a spacious flat in Merrion Square for a few years. I insisted on a big place because I needed privacy to write. I can only write behind a locked door.

Those were good times. We made a bit of money when nobody else did. It made financial sense that we would collaborate on what was becoming quite a successful series. During the day we would retreat to our separate corners to work. Me, producing my books. She, cleverly matching pictures to my words. She was good at it too. Her work flattered mine appropriately.

I became quite well known as a critic and occasional scribe for the weekend newspapers and for an infrequent guest spot on televised chat shows. In those days, everyone was more discreet and low key about their achievements, their successes. Not like current times – I can't tell you how often in the last decade I was approached about partaking in a 'reality' show. Heaven forbid. Alice avoided all of that, which suited me really. She did not like the limelight and she underestimated her own contribution to the success of my books, insisting that my work was more important, that she was just a doodler. She was timid and didn't even want it known that we were a husband and wife team in case she would be 'forced on to the telly'. Rather sweet, and it meant that for a lot of the time I could continue my life as a seemingly single man. It had its rewards. Truthfully, she could not have been a better helpmate.

Alice's mother died suddenly in 1986, at the end of our fourth year of marriage. Thanks be to God. I can't stand old people. Can't stand it even more now that I am getting to be one.

I used to make excuses to avoid visiting her and her doily-draped furniture. Used to pretend to be too busy to eat with them when she came to visit us. It was never pleasant to witness her struggling with her dentures, the half-wit dribbling by her side. Her death was a mixed blessing. We got the house. But we also got Alice's imbecilic brother. The house is quite a pile on Pembroke Avenue. The brother goes by the name of Eugene.

Alice begged me to let her keep him. Until now, that was the biggest upset in our marriage. Bad enough to have a child, but this was a 27-year-old, fifteen-stone dolt we were talking about. Eventually, I had him accommodated in a home for the 'mentally handicapped', or those with 'special needs', or whatever they are calling them this year, at considerable personal expense.

When we got engaged, I made it very clear that children were not on the agenda. Well, I said I didn't want children, and she agreed. I should have got that in writing. She must have been extraordinarily besotted with me to sacrifice something so fundamental to her in order to marry me. Maybe she thought I would change my mind, because it seems that lots of men do. Or maybe she knew that if I didn't marry her, I'd marry the next quiet one that came along.

Of course, five years into our marriage, Alice began to whinge, and grew more shrill with each passing month. I reminded her of our agreement. She claimed that at the time, that was what she had wanted too, but now she desperately wanted a child. I am nothing if not a man of my word.

I couldn't depend on her to protect herself, so I took control. I made a ritual of bedtime cocoa with a little crushed pill as an added extra. Alice thought that was so romantic.

I haven't exactly been a saint within our marriage. Women, by and large, are attracted to me and I do not like to disappoint them. Women you would never expect. Even Moya, for God's sake. I eventually resent the ones who try to cling.

In later years, I had begun to satisfy myself with some tarts that operated near the canal. I never objected to them, even before I became a client. They were objects of curiosity. They were cheaper and more desperate, mostly addicts with raddled bodies and ropey veins, but perfectly adequate for my needs. I would order them into a shower before any congress was allowed and I always provided a new toothbrush. Some of them took it for a gift. Pathetic. They are usually too emaciated to be good-looking. One would think that they might make an effort to make themselves attractive. Alas, they were only selling their various orifices; the packaging was immaterial. But still, they held a fascination for me. After all, my mother was one, or so my father said.

Returning to the house on the night Alice pushed me too far, I fumbled with the key in the door. I stepped into the dining room. She wasn't on the floor, thank God. She was sitting in the kitchen, nursing a mug of tea. Her hand rubbed at her face. She looked at me without affection. I noticed that her jaw was quite red on the right-hand side. No bruise. Yet. I looked at her. Smiled.

The wooden box in which I had locked away my darkest secrets lay open on the table in the hall, its lid agape, lock smashed, contents violated.

'Liar!' she said, her voice breaking.

It was clear that she intended to ruin me.

The second time I hit Alice, I just couldn't stop. I am very sorry about that indeed. I have been in control of my life since I was eighteen years old, and to lose control is a failing. Needless to say, I am not allowed to visit her in hospital. It is silly really. It is February 2012, so it's been three months now. In her condition, she wouldn't know if I was there or not.

It turns out that I am a violent man after all. It comes as a shock to me. I have been psychologically assessed. I decided to tell them almost everything. Apparently, I have been harbouring bitterness, resentment and frustration since my childhood. Now, there's a surprise.

What will the neighbours think? What will anybody think?

I really couldn't care less.

2. Barney

Alice O'Reilly was Avenue and we were Villas. That made all the difference in our neighbourhood. It still does. The houses on the Avenue are four times the size of ours, and their back gardens run along the gable wall of our terrace. Villas is a stupid name for our houses, as if we were somewhere foreign in the sunshine with beaches on our doorstep, when they're really only pebble-dashed council houses.

The Poshies (as we used to call them) from the Avenue didn't mix much with us. They went to different schools and hung out in different gangs, but Alice's family were different from the rest. They weren't snobby at all and didn't look down their noses like the rest of them on the Avenue. My little sister Susan used to be invited to tea in the O'Reillys', and my ma would boast about it to the other mams. I didn't pay much attention when we were nippers, but I kind of knew it was a big deal when Alice came round our house because my ma would make us polish our shoes. It used to annoy me, to be honest. As if Alice was ever going to be inspecting our shoes. She was quiet, not especially pretty and seemed sort of ordinary, if you ask me.

The mother, Breda, was quite religious and Alice wasn't allowed out that much. She was never at any of the dances or social occasions in the neighbourhood, not at ours and not at the posh tennis club ones either, so I heard. And that was probably because of Eugene. If you ask me, I'd say it was the age of the mother that caused Eugene to be the way he was. Alice's ma was the oldest of all the mothers around. She was probably forty when Alice was born, and Eugene was born four or five years after that. We didn't notice much until he got a bit older. He was about seven by the time he'd learned to walk, and his speech was strange too. I'd say that's probably why the other posh ones in the Avenue didn't want to be associating with the O'Reillys – in case poor old Eugene dribbled on their furniture. I don't remember exactly when the da died, but it wasn't long after Eugene was born. I certainly don't remember ever seeing him. The da was a civil servant of some kind, I think. High up, like. I think he was in the Land Registry office, on good money too, I'd say.

Some of the fellas in our gang used to tease Eugene and make fun of him, but Alice was always there to defend him, and somehow no one ever wanted to upset Alice. She was a strange one herself, shy and mannerly; never said boo to a goose. She seemed to spend a lot of time with her head in a book. We all thought she'd end up in the convent; there was so many nuns visiting that house that we thought the mother had plans in that direction. Susan reported that their house was full of holy pictures. Most of them had been painted by Alice. Susan had dinner there a few times; she said Alice had to spoon-feed Eugene like a baby. The food was awful, she said, everything boiled to blandness and mush. We were surprised. We thought them on the Avenue would be having cucumber sandwiches on silver plates and all. Looking at it now, I'd say the plain food was for Eugene's sake. He would never tolerate anything out of the ordinary, unless it was a biscuit or a fancy cake, but sure you'd only have them at Christmas, or if it was a birthday. Breda probably thought it was a great Catholic sacrifice for them all to make. I distinctly remember that on the rare occasion when Alice came to ours for dinner, she ate all round her and always complimented my mother on the food. Mam was delighted.

Susan and Alice were in the same class but different schools, so the odd time they'd be doing their homework together out of the same books and all. Alice definitely wasn't as smart as Susan, not going by her reports anyway. Susan was the cleverest in our family, showing me up with her As and Bs. Alice would be getting steady Cs with an A or a B in Art. If you ask me, it wasn't a lack of intelligence. She never had any time to be doing homework because looking after Eugene was a full-time job. The ma had arthritis, which got worse as she got older, but I think she realized that it wasn't fair to Alice to have her minding Eugene for the rest of her life, so she made Alice pick something to do in college. Once Alice told us that, I was pretty sure we wouldn't see much of her again. No one in the Villas ever went to college. I was kind of sorry for Susan because she was going to be losing a good pal.

Alice surprised us all by being accepted into art college. I couldn't believe she was going there of all places. Firstly, you're either good at drawing or you're not. She said it was about 'technique' and all, but if you ask me, the stuff she was drawing before she went in was as good as the stuff she drew when she finished. Nowadays, nearly all the young ones are at the coloured hair and the cross-dressing and you hardly know if they're boys or girls, and maybe that's what passes for fashion these days, but back in the seventies the art students were the only ones at that lark. Some of them were vegetarians. That says it all.

I said she wouldn't last a week, but I guess she must have got on all right, because she was there three or four years. I was wrong about her disappearing too. She still lived at home because of Eugene, and it was Susan who pulled away from the friendship more than Alice, because Susan started going out with Dave.

Alice was certainly good with her hands. I remember a sculpture thing that she made for Susan's birthday; some kind of ceramic swan-shaped yoke. I told her there and then that it was so good she could sell it. She smiled at me.

That was the first time I realized that she wouldn't be going near any convent. The smile was a bit cheeky. The years in the art college must have shaken the nun out of her. Though she still dressed very modestly, I'm not sure that she had many boyfriends, or indeed any, during her college years. Maybe those fellas scared her with their drugs and loud music.

Susan disappeared off to London after Dave within a few years and got a job as a hospital cook; married there, eventually. She never came back here to live after that. Still there now, married to DIY Dave, with four grown-up children. Chiswick. The 'w' is silent.

I had finished my apprenticeship as a mechanic and was working in my Uncle Harry's garage at that stage. I had a few bob in my pocket. I had moved into a flat in town. Had my own car. Lovely it was. A Ford Granada. It was enough to impress plenty of girls. I didn't see as much of Alice any more with Susan gone and me living in town.

13

The odd time when I called to see Mam, I would see Alice leading Eugene by the hand to the local shop. If you ask me, I'd say they did too much for him. He might have learned to fend for himself a bit more had he been let.

Mam said that Alice had some sort of job designing pictures for calendars or something like that. She said that one of the rooms in the house had been turned into a 'studio'. There were rooms in that house that hadn't been used in years, so it made sense.

Then Mam said I should ask her out. That was a bit of a shocker. She was Avenue. I was Villas. Mam said it didn't look like anyone else was ever going to ask her out, so I might as well. I don't think Mam thought we'd have any big love affair or anything; just that Alice might like the company and it would be manners. I wasn't sure myself. I was twenty-eight by then and she wasn't far behind me. She was such a quiet one, I wouldn't know what to be saying to her, and besides, I wasn't sure that we'd be able to go anywhere without Eugene, but Mam insisted, as if it would be an act of charity. But it wasn't an act of charity. Not to me. I always liked her.

When I called to the door to ask, I realized that I was nervous. That was a bit unusual for me. I can handle myself in all sorts of situations. It's just that she was a stranger to me really, though I'd known her all my life. She wasn't like the other girls I'd had a fumble with in the back of the Granada.

She answered the door herself, Eugene standing behind her in the hallway. I didn't know what words to use. I was embarrassed, like. But she smiled that smile again. Jesus, it was a lovely smile. I asked her if she'd like to come for a drive with me on Sunday, out to Killiney for a walk on the beach and then for a cup of tea in the hotel. She asked if I meant her and Eugene or just her. I said just her. She grinned then and said that would be grand and I agreed to collect her at three on Sunday.

I washed the car and had my hair cut on the Saturday. I remember because the barber nipped my left ear. Never gone back to him since. Felt like an eejit sitting in the car with Alice, making conversation, and me with a bandage on my ear. She was wearing lipstick and a brown dress with flowers on it. Very nice. Talking to her was easier than I thought it would be, though I can't remember what we talked about. Actually, I'd say she talked more than me. I got a proper look at her when we were having our tea in the hotel. Quite good-looking, but not in a film-star way. She never went blonde like the rest of them. They nearly all go blonde in the end. From being a real skinny young one, she had filled out in all the right areas, with a kind of a rounded edge to her. Not fat, mind you. Shapely, like. Her face sort of glowed whenever she smiled, and then when she'd catch me looking at her, she'd blush and twist her fingers round each other. I realized that I really did fancy her then.

She asked if I'd teach her to drive. By God, I would.

That's how it began.

The lessons were bloody terrifying. She was an atrociously bad driver. After the first lesson, I had to remove a hedge from the front grille of my car, my pride and joy. I was even more afraid for myself than I was for the car, but somehow it was worth it. She had become more relaxed with me, a bit chatty even. Still shy and all and not exactly

15

flirty or anything like that, but good fun all the same, and afterwards we would often have a coffee and some cake in a cafe. Susan wasn't wrong about her appetite.

I was sort of worried that the mother would take against me because, you know, Villas and Avenue and all that, but fair play to her, she was very nice to me and Eugene was always wanting an arm-wrestle off me. I grew fond of him as well. It wasn't his fault that he was peculiar, but he had a way of laughing like a donkey that was hilarious, even though I didn't know what he was laughing about. Neither did he, I'm sure.

At the end of her third lesson, I kissed her and asked her to marry me. She laughed but she kissed me back, so that wasn't too bad. We started having proper dates then, but she never talked about the proposal again. I think she thought I was joking, but I wasn't. I didn't have the nerve to ask her again, not for a while. I got to know her inasmuch as anyone could back then.

I think I was good for Alice, when everyone else probably thought it was the other way round. We would go to local discos and dance halls. She made herself a dress of pink silk. She said it was 'ashes of roses', but if you ask me, it was pink. We began to have a bit of fumbling, if you know what I mean, nothing too heavy. I was afraid of pushing it too much with her in case I scared her off, and I reckoned she was pretty religious like her ma. We were all a bit religious in them days, I suppose. Not like now.

We could have gone all the way once when we went to the races in Galway. We drove down in the Granada. I booked us into a small hotel for the night, in separate rooms, obviously. Alice must have been a charm because I won big on three races. I'd never had a day's luck before that. After our day out, I ordered a bottle of wine with our meal (she had seconds of everything). I wasn't used to wine then, only knew that there was red or white and that red seemed more sophisticated, so I pointed to the most expensive bottle of that on the menu (I'd had a few pints of plain already and was feeling generous). The uppity waiter asked if I was sure. I was, I said. Alice wasn't used to wine either. Within half an hour, she was talking non-sense about wanting to live in a house made of books or some such. Unusually for Alice, she began to get a bit sexy with me, a bit loose limbed. I hardly knew what to do, but then she leaned across the table in a kind of wanton way and kissed me loudly on the lips. I was in heaven, but the waiter came over and killed the moment by telling us that we were disturbing the other diners. The other diners con-sisted of a middle-aged couple and two old ladies. I think they were disturbed all right, but I didn't care.

We floated up the stairs arm in arm. I deposited her at the door of her room where we kissed passionately for a few moments. She asked if I wanted to spend the night in her room. Well, I was hardly likely to argue, was I? She flopped herself down on the bed and catapulted her shoes one after another with a steady aim towards the waste bin, missing both times by miles. My God, she was fabulous. I excused myself and ran to the bathroom at the end of the hall (well, let's just say it wasn't the Four Seasons). I stood in a plastic shower tray, soaping myself in a frenzy of prep-aration. I rinsed myself repeatedly under the trickle of lukewarm water dribbling out of the rusted shower head, and dried myself off in a fierce hurry using a towel so stiff and thin that I practically sanded myself. I threw my dressing gown around me and headed back towards the room. I caught myself in the mirror halfway down the landing. My teeth and lips were coated in reddish-grey scum from the wine. I thought that Dracula might make a better impression than me. Thundering back into the bathroom in search of my toothbrush, I skidded cartoon-style in the puddle I had left behind me and, grabbing the washbasin on the way down, landed on my right elbow with water gushing over me from the detached pipe which had come away from the wall. Jesus, the pain. And the humiliation – when I looked up to see the manager and the elderly ladies and realized that my robe had flapped open, thereby exposing me to the four winds.

To make things worse, every penny I'd won had to be paid over to the hotel and the local doctor. When I eventually got back to Alice's room at 3.30 in the morning, she was in exactly the same place as I'd left her, fully clothed but snoring lightly. I was too tired and hung-over, not to mention suffering from the pain of my newly relocated elbow, to feel anything else. I went back to my own room and had an uncomfortable night's sleep.

The journey home was horrendous. Alice was purple with embarrassment at what she saw as her disgraceful behaviour, and I couldn't drive because of my arm, which meant that she had to take the wheel. I nearly fell out of love with her on the way home. We had five near-death experiences. I thought my shoulders would be permanently lodged in my ears, and to this day I get flashbacks to that corner in Kinnegad. There was a distinct cooling of our relationship after that.

A week later, I was giving my friend Gerry the high-lights of what had happened in the hotel, showing him the hotel bill so that he could see how much the night had cost me. He took the almighty piss out of me for ordering a whole bottle of port.

Gradually, Alice and I got back to normal, though the question of spending a night together out of town was never raised again. When I eventually admitted to her that I had mistakenly ordered port instead of wine, it broke the ice and allowed us to blame the drink for the events of that night.

My mam was delighted that the two of us were going out. She often invited Alice for tea. Occasionally, Alice would bring Eugene with her and then Mam would make too big a fuss, making it awkward for me and roaring at Eugene as if he was deaf. Eugene would laugh at her. He never minded what anyone said to him.

I got on like a house on fire with Eugene. If you ask me, he was a great fella altogether really. He was a funny, happy child in a grown-up body. Always smiling. Now, I'm not saying he couldn't be difficult sometimes. For instance, he liked to dance. In public, at Mass or in the Quinnsworth usually, in front of everyone. But people understood that he was only a harmless eejit, God help him. We got into this game, him and me, where he'd be in his favourite chair and I'd come up behind him and lift up his arms and we'd pretend to be flying around the sitting room. He loved that game, so he did, and never got tired of it, and do you know what, it was a joy to be playing and to hear the laugh out of him like that. There's not many that could lift Eugene,

I can tell you. I'm as strong as an ox and he's no lightweight.

Eugene's bedtime was a lovely routine at the O'Reillys'. There'd be a pot of tea for us and a glass of milk for Eugene and a plate of buttered bread would go round. And then when it was washed up and the table scrubbed, there were prayers, everyone on their knees at the kitchen table saying the rosary, and after that Alice would read a story to Eugene, usually a fairy tale or maybe a nursery rhyme of some kind. She had a brilliant way of reading. She made all the people in the stories come alive with different voices and accents and all. I loved to listen to her almost as much as Eugene did.

After a while, Mam started quizzing me. Was I serious about Alice? Did I know what I'd be taking on? I think Mam meant well, but we had a few rows about it. It wasn't her business, after all. Mam thought it was great when I took Alice out the odd time and bought her cake, but she wanted to remind me that Alice would be responsible for Eugene when the mother died. If I married her, I'd be taking on the two of them. I made up my mind that that was fine with me. I really loved Alice by now, and if anything, Eugene would be a bonus.

Although nothing was ever said, I believed we had an understanding. We had been together for over a year. I hadn't reckoned with Oliver. Alice could be walking around now, hale and hearty, if I had reckoned with Oliver.

3. Michael

It's probably five years since I've laid eyes on Oliver Ryan, or Vincent Dax, as he is better known. I have kept an eye on his successes through the media, but the news about his savage behaviour last November is a total surprise. They say that Alice might never recover.

I first met him when we were students in University College Dublin in 1971. We were both doing an Arts degree and were in French and English together. Oliver was the type of boy that I liked to study: beautiful, in a poetic way. Obviously I was supposed to be sizing up the girls in my class, but there was something different about me.

Oliver mostly kept himself to himself, but he used to sit behind me in French lectures and we would occasionally share notes. It was only at the end of our second year that I got to know him socially. With Oliver, you only got to scratch the surface. I don't remember him ever talking about his family, for example. To this day, I don't know whether he has brothers or sisters. With all the stuff about him in the news, it's odd that even now so little has come out about his background. None of us were ever invited to his home, and he exuded a certain air that precluded questions about his private life. Oliver was a bit of a mystery really – obviously an attractive quality, which, along with his striking looks and impeccable manners, gained him a lot of attention from quite a few young ladies, not least my little sister Laura.

Laura was the star of her year. Academically gifted and stunningly beautiful in that wild West of Ireland way, I lurked in her shadow. Laura inherited our mother's good looks and Mum came from a long line of raven-haired beauties from West Cork, where once Spanish blood must have darkened the gene pool. I got my father's County Laois looks. His family had been farmers for generations. Potato farmers, and if they say you are what you eat, then the male side of our family resembled nothing if not potatoes: pale with pockmarked skin and irregular features. Everyone loved Laura.

Oliver came home with Laura to my parents' house for dinner a few times. My mother adored him to the extent that it might have put Laura off, but Laura was love-struck, although she did a terrific job of hiding it for an incredibly long time before finally yielding to Oliver's charms. Oliver and Laura were part of a gang that enjoyed trips to the pub or weekends away in our holiday home in Wicklow. She was really happy with him. I was jealous.

I have never understood what happened with Laura. Of course, she is no longer here to ask. Oliver was apparently as shocked as we were. We never got to the bottom of it. I often think about her now and what might have been. She and Oliver dated for only about five months, ending that awful summer we spent working the land in Bordeaux.

I can't remember who came up with the idea first. It might have been Laura, actually. She knew someone who knew someone, and after the rigours of a year of study and exams, we were all looking for a chance to get out of

Dublin and away from parental control. We were to plant a vineyard in France. Others would go off to canning factories in Germany and a few went to building sites in London, but the notion of a vineyard struck our ears in a singular fashion. It would surely mean access to cheap alcohol. We didn't really consider the graft part of the deal until we got there. Oliver signed up immediately, much to Laura's delight. The agreement was bed and board and a fairly meagre wage in exchange for our labour. It sounded easy and we were able to convince our parents that the opportunity to study the French language and culture should be encouraged rather than dismissed.

We arrived in the last week of May. The initial couple of weeks were exhilarating. There were acres of land we were to prepare for planting, surrounded by a large peach orchard on one side and an olive grove on the other, set on a walled estate complete with chateau in a beautifully located valley, an hour's drive from the city of Bordeaux.

Madame Véronique, a widow in her late thirties, ran the house and the estate. The only other members of the family were her six-year-old, a delightful little boy called Jean-Luc, and her elderly father, Monsieur d'Aigse. Monsieur d'Aigse and Jean-Luc were inseparable. They wandered around hand in hand, stooping to admire flowers or trees, the old man leaning down towards the boy, the little hand enclosed in his gnarled paw, which sometimes shook uncontrollably otherwise, whispering furtively and then exploding with laughter. It was never clear who was leading whom.

The d'Aigse family had owned the estate for several generations, but during the war it had been taken over by the Nazis and the family had been ejected from the premises. The vineyard that had been there previously had fallen into ruin and the livelihood of the village had been destroyed. The chateau had been stripped of its valuables, but not its majesty. The rumour was that Monsieur d'Aigse had fought in the Resistance and had directed several missions of sabotage from the vast cellars underneath the terrace steps. I don't know if that was true, but it was great to think that such exploits were being planned several floors below, while the jack-booted Nazis goose-stepped their way around the house above. There were other versions of the tale: apparently Monsieur had been horribly tortured at one stage when he had been caught smuggling a Jewish family out of the village, but it felt insensitive or inappropriate to ask about it. The war was still a living memory at that time, one that most would rather forget in that part of the world.

There were few servants as such, but there were several labourers living on the estate who seemed more than willing to help out with any job at hand. I got the impression that all the neighbours had good reason to be grateful to this noble family. This was a house of faded gentry, something we were well used to in Ireland at the time.

We lived in dormitory-style quarters, tent-like structures erected for the season in a field below the terrace, overlooked by the grand Chateau d'Aigse. We would eat with the rest of the estate workers at the communal outdoor table. The local field hands were a lively bunch from the nearby village of Clochamps and surrounding areas. They were a good-humoured bunch.

There were also some South African workers there that

summer. I had never talked to black people before, had hardly seen one in Ireland, but these boys didn't engage with us at all and kept themselves to themselves. I tried talking to them in gestures of friendship, but they kept their eyes to the ground, as if afraid. I was fascinated, I must admit. We wondered why the black guys didn't stay on the estate like the rest of us, like their white manager. I'm not sure, but I imagine they were even younger than us. Although I had attended a student rally for the Irish Anti-Apartheid Movement, I had never before encountered apartheid's ugliness. I heard that they had been sent over to learn how to plant a vineyard and take back some plants; the climate in the Western Cape was similar, apparently. I'd love to have known more about them and their circumstances, but they had very little French and virtually no English, and like everything else in those days, it was rude to ask. Their white 'manager' was an absolute prick called Joost. He had brought them to France to learn what he was too stupid and lazy to learn himself. He did no work and instead spent his day drinking and shouting instructions at them, physically beating them if they made a mistake. He tried to ingratiate himself with the rest of us by making crude jokes about his countrymen's colour and stupidity. France was a country still recovering from its own shame about sitting back and allowing the segregation and persecution of the Jews, and the locals were not going to let that happen again. We all protested to Madame, who eventually was forced to eject them from the estate.

The accommodation was quite basic: a dorm for men and one for women, each with a water pump and hole-in-the-ground toilet at the end. Not the sort of thing we would put up with now, indeed, but our standards were that bit lower when we were young. We thought it was all amusingly exotic.

The work, however, was gruelling to begin with, before we all toughened up, and in fact by the end of June there was little to be done on the vines and we moved to the orchard and olive grove, where the work was considerably less taxing. I spent the first month hoeing beneath each vine, scraping out each weed from the clover, grass and wild oats that covered the rows between vines. It was remarkable how fast they grew in early June, an inch or two a day sometimes, though Madame told us that the growth spurts were even faster in the early spring. Oliver and Laura were put with a different team on the vital task of *épamprage*, removing the unwanted sucker shoots from the vine trunk and selectively removing shoots from the head. The vines were cared for like ailing children, monitored, encouraged, soothed and coaxed into grapefulness.

I must admit that we took full advantage of the free wine after work and would often crawl into bed in the smallest hours of the morning, blind drunk. In fact, some people didn't make it as far as their own bed. Sometimes they only made it as far as other people's beds. Such a heady time.

And yet, I knew I had to try to fix the thing that was wrong with me. I was on a mission to rid myself of the albatross that was my virginity. I thought that it might cure me. Sharing a bunk-house with those immodest men was quite a strain.

Oliver's spoken French was far better than Laura's or

mine, and he often negotiated between Madame and 'les Paddies', as we became known. It was because of this that old Monsieur d'Aigse began to take an interest in Oliver. He asked Oliver the English names for certain plants and flowers, and Oliver would obligingly translate. Before long, Oliver was promoted. He spent more and more time in the chateau in Monsieur's study. Officially, Monsieur took him on as a translator, working on some old maps or some such that Monsieur had compiled for his private collection. Lucky bastard. The vineyard work was tough. Oliver didn't move out of the dorm, but he no longer had to work in the field. Laura was a little disgruntled about it, I remember. Occasionally, I spied him from the field beside the lower lake, sitting outside on the terrace with Monsieur, a jug of wine by his side, or playing some high-jinks game with the highly mischievous Jean-Luc. Their shouts and laughter ricocheted off the walls of the house and echoed through the valley. Oliver looked like the missing link between the old man and the boy. We noted how well Oliver seemed to fit in with them. When he came back to us in the evenings, he was like a different man. More content, perhaps; happier, anyway. Laura wasn't the only one who was jealous of the time that Oliver spent with the family. I, too, didn't like the way he became more like one of them than us. Instinctively, I knew that Oliver could never love me, but at least while he was dating Laura, I could be around him, in his circle of friends. Now, he was becoming removed from us. He would return full of stories about the funny things that Jean-Luc said, the new game they had played together. Oliver told us at one stage that if he ever had a son, he wanted him to be just like Jean-Luc. I lightly commented that Monsieur d'Aigse would be a good father figure too, but Oliver just glared at me for a second before walking off. Whatever the story was with Oliver's parentage, it was clearly a sore point. I didn't know then that he was violent, but he certainly looked like he wanted to hit me.

4. Oliver

When I left school, women were a complete mystery to me – at least until I met Laura Condell. I had been in the sole company of priests and boys as a boarder in St Finian's since I was six years old, and apart from one summer on Stanley Connolly's farm, where, quite frankly, his three feline sisters terrified me, I had no experience of women. Apparently, you are supposed to learn the facts of life and the etiquette of how to treat women from your mother, or, failing that, your father. I learned instead by osmosis.

Particular magazines, carefully camouflaged in parcels containing biscuit tins or woollen jumpers, were passed among the boys of St Finian's and treated as hard currency. The source was usually a boy's English cousin or foreign friend. My time with the magazines was severely limited due to my financially straitened circumstances. Not having much bargaining power, I did not get many chances to assess their content. I was naturally aroused and very curious about these images, the slender legs, the soft look of their breasts, and the beautiful curve of the hip from buttocks to waist.

When I eventually got to see the real thing, I was not too disappointed. The women in the magazines in those days were not very unlike their actual counterparts. I think modern pornography is probably the single biggest cause of erectile dysfunction. How else is a poor teenager to react when he finally gets to grips with an un-depilated female body that is unlikely to have globe-shaped breasts standing to attention, a tiny waist and a bronzed oily sheen that he might think would help to slide himself inside her? The disillusionment with the reality must have a physical effect. Of course, now they can take a pill for that. I never needed such assistance.

I was, naturally, interested in sex, but I regarded boys with girlfriends as rather suspicious. Apart from sex, what would one want with a girl?

I knew, partly from a purple-faced biology teacher and partly from filthy innuendo disseminated by the other boys, that women bled regularly, and it seemed disgusting to me. Alien. I made it clear to Alice throughout our marriage that I did not want to know of cycles or bleeding or cysts or discharges or any of the other revolting parapher-nalia that seems to come with the gender, and to be fair to her, she has left me untroubled by it all. A monthly 'head-ache' is tolerable to me, and if she had to go into hospital for a little 'procedure' now and then, what of it? Dear Alice.

At a school dance in the winter of my last year of school, I managed to shove my tongue into a girl's mouth. Word had it that she'd let you ride her if you bought her a lemonade. Two boys had claimed success by this method. Later, outside on the bonnet of Purple-Face's car, while couples danced inside to Dana's 'All Kinds of Everything', my hands first encountered female breasts; 'boozums', as they were known in the school patois. She made it difficult for me. I was forced to beg. How curiously yielding they were, falling around my desperate fingers; without their upholstery, pendulous and weighty. She allowed me to kiss them and suddenly it all became deadly serious and I tried to concentrate on my breathing to prevent the impending climax in my unfashionable trousers, but as my hands began to wander southwards, she prissily slapped me away with the, I suspect, well-rehearsed line: 'A girl has to draw the line somewhere and my line is drawn around my waist.'

She pushed me away from her and reorganized her bra and vest and shirt and sweater and coat (it was winter), and I felt upset and confused and tried to kiss her again and get her to reconsider, but she complained it was cold and walked back into the hormone-drenched hall. I wanted to follow her and to apologize, but I was not sure what I had done wrong, just that she had made me *feel* wrong, and bad. Not knowing what else to do, I burst into tears and masturbated and cursed the little cow, and felt better. My first pre-sexual sexual encounter. I should have reckoned with the braggadocio of the schoolboy. It was clear to me that nobody had ever broached her second line of defence.

A year later, when I first started having sexual relationships with the girls in college, I was far more successful. While the 'sexual revolution' of the 1960s had somehow just bypassed Ireland, in 1971 there were enough girls around campus with the curiosity and education to know that they also were entitled to orgasm. They were ready to do the things they'd read about. I followed the American tradition of hitting the four bases in order. I think I was unusual in that I almost always got to fourth base, and this certainly quickly boosted my confidence. Some of the other fellows subtly asked for advice, cloaking the request in jokey banter, but there was no secret.

I have learned over the years how to charm them. It's not too hard if you are handsome and can appear to be clever with a dry wit. Act as if you haven't noticed them. Then, gradually, begin to take an interest, as if she is a specimen in a laboratory. Poke her a bit with a long stick while keeping your distance. Ignore her for long periods to see how she reacts and then give her a good shake. It almost always works.

In college, I dated girls until they yielded, but usually dropped them when they began to ask questions about my background or my family. My reputation was one of a mysterious loner, and women, being naturally nosey, all thought they could get to the bottom of it. Perhaps they all thought they could mother me? As I did not have a mother, it was all meaningless to me. I fell into a pattern: pursue, claim, conquer, move on. It amazed me how women would try to possess me as soon as we'd slept together, as if I owed them a part of me. I had never had women in my life, and I simply did not know what to do with them. One girl, who I left snivelling in her pre-dawn bed, threw a mug at my head and called me a 'bastard'. I took my revenge by sleeping with her twin sister the following night.

Some of the girls I liked more than others. I certainly did not hate women, but I can't say that I felt an emotional connection to any of them. Except for Laura.

Laura was a challenge from day one. The first time I saw her, she was crossing the campus with two other girls. It was a cold day, and I noted their breath wisping into the air as they laughed and chatted. She was wearing a home-knitted red woollen scarf around her neck and a long trench coat. She waved at me and smiled and I was caught for a moment, captured by her vivacity and unsure of how to respond, and then Michael, with whom I was walking, called out to her and I realized that she was waving at him, and I felt foolish.

Michael Condell introduced Laura as his sister, and I admit to being taken aback that siblings could look so different.

Ironic, when you think about it.

After that, I made a point of seeking her out, but unlike the other girls, she took no particular interest in me. Laura was darkly beautiful, wilful and spirited, impulsive and brave. She was a year behind me, reading French, Philosophy and Politics. She dated the rugby boys, the rich boys who had their own cars. It was going to be hard for me to compete, but, as I made an effort to get to know her, at least on the periphery, I realized that I didn't just want to sleep with her. I wanted her in my life. I hoped that the golden aura that surrounded her might somehow encompass me and lift me to her pedestal. I can't even now put my finger on what it was that was different about Laura. I had been out with beautiful girls before who all failed to tug at my alleged heartstrings. It may have been the way her blue eyes sparkled when she laughed, or the way she walked with purpose. It could have been her confidence, the fact that she seemed so sure of her place in the world when the rest of us were just pretending.

My usual tactics did not work with Laura. She appeared not to notice me at all. I was conscious of my second-hand clothes and my squalid bedsit, and knew I would have to reinvent my story if I was to stand a chance, so I befriended Michael and began to curry favour that way. I was invited to their home for dinners and sat across the table from Laura, ignoring her and pretending to be riveted by her mother's conversation, feigning fascination in her father's rhododendrons. When oblique questions were asked about my parentage, I deflected them, hinting at a father who was always travelling abroad on important but unspecified business. I hinted at a country house that I might one day inherit and was vague and enigmatic enough to discourage further questioning. Still, Laura paid me no heed.

I changed my game, and instead began to pay her some attention, included her in our plans, took an interest in her course work, offered help with essays and invited her for drinks with us. Sometimes I would try subtly to ask Michael about her, but he would react huffily. Jealous of my interest in her, I assume. Michael was as gay as Christmas. It was never mentioned or acknowledged. Later, in France, I tried to help him be straight. Back in the day, we genuinely thought it might be possible. Perhaps we knew it wasn't, but we were not willing to accept it. He liked me. I did not mind. He was useful. I liked him too, but not in the way that I know he wanted. However, his fraternal connection to Laura allowed me to get closer to her, although she was still proving immune to every seduction ploy I knew.

Eventually, inspired by Rostand's *Cyrano de Bergerac*, which we were studying at the time, I decided to send her a love letter. I wrote more drafts of this letter than I have of any of my books. There were flowery versions, there was a terrible one in my own rhyming verse entirely ripped

34

off from Keats, there was a version which included a Shakespearian sonnet, but in the end I simply told her how I felt about her, how beautiful I thought her, how she made me smile and that I hoped she might one day let me take her to dinner. Above everything I have ever written, that letter is the text of which I am most proud. It was honest.

Two days after I posted the letter, I exited the lecture theatre to find that Laura was waiting for me. She hooked her arm into mine, wrapped her red scarf around both of our necks and gave me a chaste kiss on the cheek. I loved her then, I think, if that warm and giddy feeling is love.

Our courtship was slow and sweet and delicate. I let Laura dictate the pace of our relationship. On a practical level, I had to deflect her curiosity about my background and lied that I lived with a strict aunt, which negated the possibility of her visiting my home, but Laura was not interested in my home, my past, my parents. Now that Laura had decided that we were a pair, she was interested in me. Me. We became quite the golden couple in a few short months and I basked in the sunlight she reflected upon me. I was no longer the grubby boy in the second-hand coat trying to get his leg over.

When we did eventually make love, it was entirely different from anything I had experienced before. It was an early March afternoon in her parents' house and a wintry sun cast shadows across the tiled kitchen floor as we drank tea from china cups, leaning back, side by side, against the Aga oven. We were talking about our plans for the summer and Laura suggested that we needed to get out of Dublin, 'to get some privacy', she said, and looked quickly at me, fiercely, and then looked away again. I knew what she meant, but I teased her – 'Privacy? For what?' – and I brushed a strand of her dark hair out of her eyes and kissed her mouth gently. She responded softly at first and then twirled and stood in front of me so that we were nose to nose. 'They won't be back until after four,' she said, and led me by the hand up the back stairs to her bedroom. Once there, we quickly stripped and dived under the covers, both of us shy and tentative, and there we stayed for the next two hours, tenderly touching and tasting, and as I moved inside her I thought, idiotically, that life was good and that all would be well.

Maybe I fooled myself. I thought I loved her and was loved by her and we were real, proper, grown-up people with genuine emotions and feelings for each other, and while in the past it may have given me satisfaction that others were jealous of us, now I simply wished that everyone could have what we had. Laura made me good, and I could never imagine a time when my love for her could be displaced by anybody. I was terribly immature.

If only we hadn't gone to France that summer of 1973.

Nine years later, I met Alice. She was no Laura, but by then I knew that I never deserved a girl like Laura. Alice was simple, loyal, discreet and kind. Alice was a haven from my nightmares. I have never felt the same passion for Alice that I had for Laura, but until three months ago we made a very good life together. Alice and I complemented each other.

It was no challenge to take Alice from Barney Dwyer. He was clearly one of life's losers, punching outrageously above his weight by dating Alice. I am still mystified as to what she saw in him. Do I feel bad about usurping him? Not really. All is fair in love and war, isn't it? Of course not. That is the biggest and most pernicious lie ever. How ridiculous. Nothing is fair in love and life, and I have wasted far too much of my time wishing it were not so.

I imagine Alice's expectations were low, so it was remarkably easy to overwhelm her, seduce her, marry her. She yielded easily. Barney never stood a chance. I was better than him. He knew it.

Naturally, everyone expected me to have a wife who was more gregarious, more 'showbiz', somebody like Laura perhaps, but they do not know me. Nobody knows me. I chose Alice.

5. Barney

We'd been going out together for about ten months and Alice was doing some flora and fauna illustrations for some nature books. They were very nice, very detailed. She took so much care with her work, examining every tiny vein in every leaf under a microscope in her back room. She was very dedicated indeed. Then her publisher gave her a bound rough copy of a children's book to read and that was it.

I was there the first time she read it to Eugene. There was a bit about a flying chair in it, and because I had started that game with Eugene, he straight away was hooked on it. He wanted her to read it again immediately afterwards. And again. She thought it was wonderful, and it certainly meant a huge amount to her that it appealed to Eugene.

If you ask me, it was just all right. Even now that the books have sold all over the world, I still think they are just all right. The author's name was on the cover, Vincent Dax. But when we were introduced to him, he told us his real name was Oliver Ryan. I didn't get that. If it were me, I'd have wanted everyone to know that it was me who'd written them.

I was there the night they met in March 1982; I'll never forget it. We were at the launch of the nature book that Alice had illustrated. I always hated those nights because we'd have to dress up and I'd be wearing my suit which was a bit tight and a tie which nearly choked me. Oliver was one of those confident types of guys, in a proper posh linen suit, smoking a French cigarette, tanned and good-looking. He looked like a film star with his dark eyes and his suit. I was standing beside Alice when we were introduced, and I swear I don't think he even saw that I was there. He was looking at her, I mean really looking at her, and she was doing that cute blushing thing she does. So I pretended to cough but I accidentally made a kind of vomit sound instead, and then I got his attention and he turned towards me, so I put my arm around her shoulder, to give him the hint that she was mine and that he shouldn't be chatting her up. It was a foolish move. I'd never done it before, we weren't that type of couple, so my hand just dangled embarrassingly over her left breast and she sort of squirmed. She introduced me as her boyfriend, Barney. I was beginning to feel a bit better, but then he said he had a friend who had a dog called Barney and she laughed, a sort of light, tinkly laugh that I hadn't heard before, and then he laughed. They were laughing together. So I laughed too, or pretended to, but it sounded fake. If the scene had been in a comic book, the speech bubble coming from my head would have said, 'Guffaw guffaw.'

I took up smoking. It took me a while to get used to it. I tried to get a tan that summer, but the tops of my ears just burned and I looked stupid. Oliver was really good for Alice's career though. She did the illustrations for his first book, and it seemed like there could be a few sequels. He took us out to dinner a few times, usually with a few other couples, old college friends of his, I suppose. They were very nice, but I didn't feel that I had much in common with them. For some reason, they seemed a lot younger than me, and at the same time more grown-up, like. They'd be talking about books I hadn't read and films I hadn't seen or politics I'd no interest in. Some of them had been away together on the Continent years earlier. Like Cliff Richard in that film, only not in a bus.

At the end of that May, there was talk of another trip abroad to a Greek island. Apart from the fact that I didn't own a passport, it was out of the question for me. Uncle Harry had had a mild stroke earlier in the year and was leaving a lot of the workload on my shoulders. Not that I minded. He had been very good to me and my mam. But to be honest, travel wasn't really my cup of tea. I don't take the sun that well, and I was nervous around foreigners. To be truthful, imaginary flying is as far as it goes for me. I could tell that Alice really wanted to go, but it seemed just as impossible for her. Her mother was a bit frail and would definitely not be in favour of such an escapade, and there was also Eugene to consider. She couldn't have managed on her own.

It was my idea. I went to Alice's mother myself and suggested it. I would come by every day before work and help Eugene get washed and dressed and bring him to the remedial centre where he spent his days. Mrs O'Reilly would collect him herself and then I'd come over after dinner and help get him settled, take him on a quick imaginary flight in the chair, read him a story and get him into bed. She wasn't too pleased by the idea initially, but I eventually managed to persuade her that Alice deserved a break after all her years of minding the mad fella. We broke the news to Alice together. I was very proud of myself. I don't go out of my way to do a lot of things that aren't in some way for me, but I was doing this for Alice and, I suppose, so that she knew how much I loved her, without me having to say it. I'm useless at that soppy stuff.

Those three weeks were the longest of my entire life. Eugene was no problem. He whimpered a bit at bedtime because I didn't read the stories like Alice did, but he really was very good. I missed Alice myself, more than I thought I would. So much so that two days before she was due back, I shut up the garage early and took myself into the Happy Ring House on O'Connell Street and bought a diamond engagement ring. I'd been saving up a long time, without really knowing it myself, and the fella in the shop was very helpful. It wasn't a massive diamond, just a small flat one on a thin gold band. The fella in the shop said it was discreet. I think that's probably polite for small.

I was expecting her back on the Saturday night. I was all prepared to go and collect her, but her mother said one of the gang was giving her a lift home from the airport. By Sunday evening she still hadn't rung. The engagement ring in its velvet box was burning a hole in my pocket. I decided to go round.

Mrs O'Reilly answered the door. I remember thinking how lucky it was when she put me in the formal sitting room and told me Alice would be with me shortly. I didn't want to propose over the kitchen table in front of Eugene and the mammy.

When Alice came in and avoided looking at me, suddenly I knew there was something terribly wrong. Even though her eyes were red-rimmed from crying, she looked beautiful to me then. Her skin was a kind of goldy-brown and her hair was lightened auburn by the sun. She had freckles I'd never seen before. For a minute, I felt that it was all going to be OK, that whatever was wrong could be solved by the box in my pocket.

'Barney,' she said, 'I'm sorry.'

I knew instantly by the way she said it that she meant she was sorry *for me*. She was apologizing to me. How stupid could I have been? I felt an instant pain deep in my gut. I was actually winded. Somebody else. Oliver. Alice and Oliver. I had delivered her into his arms to prove how much I loved her.

'Oliver,' I said. Not a question.

Why in the name of Jesus didn't I cop that sooner? He was hardly inviting us out to dinner for my company. I'd thought it was to do with work, but how could it have been when they rarely discussed work on those nights out? Still, even if I had guessed he liked her, I'd never have thought that she was into him. She was *my* girlfriend, after all.

The Happy Ring House wouldn't give me my money back. I ended up swapping it for a brooch for Mam's birthday a few months later. For a long time, I was very sad about the whole thing. I had had it all planned, you see, down to the three children and the extra room I would build on to our house for Eugene with his own record player so he could dance when he wanted. I hadn't thought of a future without Alice. I was raging with jealousy and wondered if they'd slept together already. Probably. Oliver was some operator, but I fecking helped him. I couldn't bear to see either of them for months after that. A couple of weeks after we split, I removed the spark plugs from Oliver's car when I saw it parked outside Alice's. And then, like a smack, in December I got a wedding invitation in the post with a note attached from Alice, saying she'd perfectly understand if I didn't want to come, that she'd always be fond of me and that she'd never forget my kindness to her and Eugene.

Mam made me go. 'Hold your head up high,' she said, 'and don't let that snobby bitch think that you're not good enough.' I'd never heard her say the word 'bitch' before, but Mam took it as hard as I did myself. I'm sure she'd thought we were going up in the world. I never thought Alice was a bitch.

The wedding was quite small. Oliver had no family there. I thought that was peculiar myself. Maybe he hadn't got family, but it's unusual not to even be able to rustle up an uncle or a cousin. They didn't go for the big fancy hotel reception. I was grand until they exchanged vows in the church, and then I went to pieces. Susan and DIY Dave took me out and gave me a proper talking to. Then there was a good dinner in a restaurant in town owned by some gay fella friend of Oliver's. I don't know how I made it through the meal. I probably wouldn't have gone at all if I'd known it was such a small wedding. I wasn't really able to get lost in the crowd. I did get to chat to Alice on our own for a bit. She looked gorgeous and I told her so. She tried to tell me that I'd meet the right person one day. I smiled and nodded and wished her and Oliver the best.

It annoyed the shite out of me that Oliver never

even saw me as competition. He never acknowledged me as Alice's boyfriend, or ex-boyfriend. I was beneath him. That's how he made me feel back then. I know better now.

Mrs O'Reilly said I'd always be welcome in their house, and Eugene said he missed me and he was sorry if he'd done something bad and could we be friends again. I swear that fella would break your heart. They should have explained it to him, instead of treating him like an eejit. I did call in to the house after that, and I'd take Eugene out for a drive on the odd Sunday. I even taught him a few things. I think Alice and her ma had stopped trying with Eugene after a certain point, but I didn't see any reason not to try and help him, so after a few months with me, he could eat his own dinner with a spoon if I cut up the food for him, and he learned to wipe his chin after I gave him a 'magic' handkerchief. Mrs O'Reilly was delighted with me. She told me one night that she thought Alice had made a mistake with Oliver, but as soon as she'd said it, she tried to unsay it. I suppose she felt it wouldn't help anyone to say it, but I was glad because it helped me.

The reality is that Oliver had money and style. He was becoming an internationally successful writer, and I was a mechanic with a sideline in second-hand cars back living with my mam in the Villas. She needed a bit of looking after, and Susan had gone. I was never in a university in my life. Oliver, the bollix, would treat her right, I thought, even if he was a bit high and mighty. They moved into town after they married and so we didn't see each other for a few years, but when Mrs O'Reilly died, they moved back into her family home with Eugene and I'd see them around the place. They got friendly with that one off the telly who'd since moved in next door to them, Moya Blake. That seemed to settle it for me. Moya was totally Avenue and they were her new mates. Lah-di-dah, if you know what I mean. It's not like they ignored me though. Oliver usually nodded and Alice looked guilty, but eventually there was a bit of a thaw. I tried not to bear a grudge. It was fecking hard work, I can tell you.

I had to keep my distance from Eugene then. I explained that Alice was home now to mind him and I wouldn't be calling in any more. I thought he understood. Oliver and Alice never had children. That was strange. I always thought Alice would be a great mum, but I supposed she wasn't able to or something. She was no longer any of my business and I never asked.

The one thing I could never figure out was that they sent Eugene away to live in St Catherine's on the far side of town. I was really, really shocked at that. Alice didn't give me much of an explanation when I asked, but John-Joe in Nash's told me on the QT that Oliver had said Eugene had become very difficult after the mother died, and they had no choice but to put him in a home. I would still have the craic with him when I saw him on the road, but he'd put on a fierce amount of weight and looked a bit miserable. Still, I'd never have thought they'd put him in a home. If you ask me, that's a great shame. I called in a few times and offered to take him out for the day from the home, but Oliver warned me that I should just forget about him and that asking after him just upset Alice. Oliver said it wasn't a good idea to go and visit him, that he wouldn't recognize me and might get aggressive with me. The poor fella, I couldn't believe he'd do that, but Oliver insisted and, I must admit, at the time I thought Oliver knew about things more than I did myself.

I never imagined that I'd be able to hold Alice's hand again, or·that I'd have Eugene back in my life, but it's a funny old world and no mistake.

6. Michael

By the time we were in France, I was terrified of my homo-sexuality but had convinced myself that it was a phase I could grow out of. Even though I had never envisioned my future as a happily married father, I had always assumed that I *would* get married, father some children and do what was expected of me. But that summer, it became impossible to keep my true desires buried. I wanted Oliver. But I couldn't tell him. Homosexuality in Ireland wasn't decriminalized until 1993.

My bunk was next to his in the dorm. I knew when he was sneaking out to meet my sister in the night. To my shame, I once followed them and watched as the moonlight glanced off the contours of their graceless humping. Not at all what I had expected. I had read *Lady Chatterley's Lover* twice. Well, some of it. I had gleaned that sex was an earthy kind of thing, but somehow in my mind I expected it to be balletic. In reality, it looked base and animalistic. Definitely more Joyce (I had read bits of that too) than Lawrence. I felt like quite the pervert; firstly feeling lust for a *man*, and secondly watching my *sister* in the act. Shame on me.

It seems obvious, looking back now, that they must have known I was gay. I wasn't particularly camp in my behaviour, but my obvious lack of interest in the local damsels might have aroused some suspicion. On a stifling night towards the end of July, after several jugs of the local wine and a few puffs of a sweet-smelling cigarette from one of the locals, I could contain myself no longer. We were playing an old innocent childish game of Truth or Dare, although we had rechristened the game 'Truth or Drink'. When asked a direct personal question, one had to either answer honestly or drink two fingers of wine from the jug. It was once again my turn, and one of the girls asked which of them I would like to kiss. I think now it might have been a leading question. There was an expectant hush as they awaited my response. Around the brazier, in front of all gathered, I threw my arms around Oliver with abandon (gay) and wildly declared to the assembly, 'I am in love with Oliver!'

Laura smacked me in the face. Oliver laughed. His laughter hurt me more than the slap. Laura pulled me out of the tent, cursing my drunkenness. She was absolutely furious with me, insisting that I was making an utter fool of myself. I couldn't be a gay. Dad would kill me. It was immoral. Father Ignatius would be scandalized. What was Oliver going to think? Et cetera, et cetera.

I don't remember going to bed that night, but the next morning I woke in my bunk early with a sense of horror, fear and shame. I turned towards Oliver. He was lying on his back, hands behind his head, facing me.

'Don't be a queer,' he said. 'I dislike queers, filthy bastards.'

I turned away in misery and blinked furiously to keep the tears at bay.

'You just haven't found the right woman yet. You need

the ride. That's all that's wrong with you. Bloody virgin. Leave it to me. I'll get you fixed up.'

He bounded out of bed, reached over and tousled my hair, and flicked his towel towards my arse underneath my sweat-drenched sheet. If he was trying to turn me off him, he was doing a spectacularly bad job. I decided to go along with the charade, however. After all, Oliver disliked queers.

Oliver pointed out that Madame Véronique was a widow. Widows, he said, were notoriously 'sex-mad'. Plus, she was French, and therefore sexy. He didn't think that the fact she was twice my age should be an impediment. Oliver encouraged me to get closer to her. Offer to help out in the kitchen at mealtimes, compliment her on her clothing, her hair, and so on. Ludicrous, I know, but it meant I could confide in Oliver, spend time with him.

Unsurprisingly, Madame was utterly baffled by my attentions. But what a marvellous woman! She taught me everything I know. In the kitchen.

She aroused my palate if nothing else. Ireland in those days was a gastronomic wilderness. Parsley sauce was considered the height of sophistication. Here, I learned that boiling was not the only way to treat a vegetable; that pastry was an artist's medium; that meat could be smoked, cured, grilled and braised; that herbs and spices added flavour; and that garlic existed.

My culinary education started by accident. Literally. When I presented myself at the kitchen door offering assistance that first morning, I witnessed the very event that was to shape my future. Anne-Marie, the elderly kitchen helper, tripped and fell on her way to the sink while carrying a large tray of freshly made brioche, breaking her right arm in the process. It wasn't a terribly bad break – there were no bones piercing skin or anything like that – but it was obviously painful. She yelped in agony and an enormous fuss ensued. The doctor from the village was sent for. Anne-Marie was brought to the local hospital and we didn't see her again for the duration of our stay. As I was already on the scene, and the show had to go on, Madame demonstrated what needed to be done with the brioche (sprinkle with water and pop into the oven), and seconded me to kitchen duties for the rest of the week. What bliss. I was a quick learner, and by the end of that day I had prepared my first vinaigrette, steamed six fresh trout (steamed!), roasted a sack of carrots and sautéed some courgettes. Of course, it was some time before I could whip up a sauce *velouté* or produce my own peach *barquettes*, but I took to it like a *canard à l'eau*. Madame was an excellent teacher, but, if I may say so, I was an excellent student. Besides, I was indoors doing work I actually enjoyed, and though the heat could be monstrous with two ovens going, it was still better than sweating it out in the fields.

When I came back to the dorm that night, I was glowing with excitement. Oliver assumed that Madame had piqued my interest, but in fact I had completely forgotten that my mission was to seduce her.

Of course, Laura was furious: her brother was living it up in the kitchen; her boyfriend was leading an even more refined life in the library; and there she was, a mere *paysanne*. I tried to pacify her by telling her how well she looked. The physical work was toning her nicely, and once she had got past the broiled-face thing, she had developed quite a tan and was beginning to resemble a diminutive

Amazonian warrior. She didn't accept the compliment graciously, but complained continually of feeling tired and excluded. To my eternal regret, I paid little attention to her plight.

I made a few pathetic attempts to flirt with Madame, but she remained as unconvinced as I was. The language barrier made it that bit more awkward (as if it wasn't futile enough), but I was determined not to disappoint Oliver. He gave me a few tips and I had my instructions.

At the end of one particularly hot and sweaty day, I brushed Madame's hair out of her face and asked if I might comb it for her. Oliver insisted it was a guaranteed winner of a move. She was a little taken aback, but assented. Oliver was right. Women love their hair to be handled. As I was combing her hair, I had a marvellous idea. Madame's hair was quite long. I took a thick strand in one hand and began to weave it into another strand so that it was sort of knotted on the top of her head. *Très chic*. I had just invented a hairstyle. How stereotypical of me. It was actually a 'chignon', a typical French style popular in Paris in the forties, but how were we to know? I had never played with a woman's hair before, and Madame may have known her *bain-marie* from her *sabayon*, but she was bloody hopeless in the style department. Still, she was no fool.

'*Tu es homosexuel?*' she said.

Luckily, the word translated very easily.

'*Oui*,' I said. And then I cried for an hour.

Madame was terribly sweet about it all. I haven't a damn clue what she was saying, but there was much miming of finger to lips to reassure me that she would keep my secret. She wasn't at all perturbed by the news; didn't have me thrown out, didn't laugh at me, wasn't horrified. It all fell into place for her. A mystery was solved. Via sign language, I admitted that I was in love with Oliver, and that scandalized her a bit all right. She knew, as everyone did, that Oliver and my sister Laura were an item. She gave me a maternal hug and said a lot of stuff in French while gesticulating up the hill. I think she meant that I should go for a walk. I did. It didn't help.

That night, back in the dorm, Oliver was eager to know how the seduction was going.

'Grand,' I said.

The daily struggle continued. Madame would catch me watching Oliver at the centre of his new family with Monsieur and the boy. Bad enough to have my own sister as competition, but now I had Madame Véronique's family too. I wondered if she was also jealous of the time her father and son spent with Oliver. She would smile sympathetically, but then thrust her comb into my hands. I suppressed my jealousy, buried myself in my new role and learned as much as I could in the kitchen.

A couple of days later, Madame introduced me to Maurice, a burly odd-looking vegetable producer who owned a farm at the top of the hill. Maurice's English was better than Madame's. He intimated that Madame had told him I was *un homo*. He said he was also gay and that he could bring me to a nightclub in Bordeaux where I could meet other gay men. I was puce with embarrassment, but he laughed heartily and took me away to be deflowered by the divine Thierry – a cross-dressing pig farmer from Saint-Émilion. The scales fell from my eyes that night. I realized that I belonged to this strange community. I fitted into this world. I still have dreams about waking up beside Thierry.

I arrived late the next morning for my kitchen duties. Madame winked and grinned and made some obscene gestures with her hands. What a truly wonderful woman! Of course, Oliver was full of questions about where I'd been. I made up something, but he knew that I hadn't been with Madame, and I could feel his disappointment in me. Yet his disapproval of my homosexuality, which had previously so bothered me, now mattered not a jot. My feelings for Oliver had changed overnight. My sexual interest in him would never be reciprocated; what would be the point, after all? He figured out where I'd been, and moved his bunk to the other side of the dorm. Still, nothing was said. Laura was more accepting now that I had taken my eye off Oliver. In fact, she went out of her way to help me with my assignations, arranging lifts to the city for me and introducing me to other men she suspected of being gay. My summer took off in a completely hedonistic way, which now seems horribly inappropriate in light of the tragedy that was to come.

By mid August, Laura was still complaining of exhaustion, much to the annoyance of the other workers. Everybody had complained in the beginning, but by now they were all used to it. Laura must have been quite isolated in retrospect, her brother and her boyfriend working in the house while she laboured in the fields. There were others in our group, of course, but she was closer to us than to anybody else. I was now far too busy with my new life to notice much about my little sister, though it was clear that her relationship with Oliver was fizzling out. He was spending less and less time with her and more time with the old man and the boy. Then, one day, she was carried into the kitchen in a state of collapse and was brought to the doctor. Madame, as usual, took control. Oliver and I were worried, but Madame later explained to Oliver that Laura had a gastric complaint, that she would be right as rain after a week's rest. She was installed in a turret room of the chateau, up two floors via a rickety wooden staircase. I looked in on her a few times a day. She was uncommunicative and tearful. I guessed that her relationship with Oliver wasn't going well, but honestly I couldn't blame him if he'd begun to lose interest. Her constant complaining had begun to grate on everyone's nerves. I tried to gently broach the subject, but she didn't want to know, saying that I 'just wouldn't understand'. She was right. I still don't.

I tried to talk to Oliver. He maintained that Laura was simply jealous of our working conditions compared to hers. He admitted that he had tried to finish their relationship, but said that Laura found it hard to accept that it was over. He claimed his work for Monsieur simply took up too much time and that Laura resented it.

It seemed clear to me that while Oliver might have loved Laura once, his love for his new 'family' overshadowed that completely. Oliver chose to spend time with them rather than with her. I raised this carefully with Laura and suggested that she just give Oliver some time. It wasn't as if he was going to stay with them for ever. We would all be returning to Ireland soon enough, and although it was a strange infatuation, could she not see that it was just temporary?

Laura declared it was over, that she had no choice but to accept Oliver's rejection of her, but refused to discuss it further. I thought there was more to it than that, but I didn't push the issue. And then circumstances overwhelmed us to such a degree that Laura's erratic moods were pushed to the back of my mind.

Three weeks later, the day after the harvest had started in earnest, we were all fast asleep in our dorms. Everybody was particularly exhausted as all hands were on deck that day. My kitchen duties and Oliver's admin ones were suspended, as there was a short enough window in which to pick the first harvest of grapes at their best. In a shattered state, I collapsed on to my bunk that night but woke some hours later in a state of disorientation. There were raised voices coming from outside. Oliver and Laura were shouting at each other, though, to be truthful, Laura was the one doing the shouting. Others stirred, and some went out to see what was going on. I had really had enough of Laura's mood swings. She was just humiliating herself, and Oliver, and me. When I got outside, he was physically trying to remove her arms from around his neck. 'You do love me! You have to!' she was sobbing, refusing to let go.

'Laura!' I called out to her sharply. She let him go then and turned to glare at me.

'Go to bed, Laura,' I whispered fiercely, 'you're making a show of yourself.'

Oliver turned, as if to walk away from me, but I stopped him. 'Oliver, we need to have a conversation.' He looked uncertain but followed me back into the bunk-house, and gradually everybody settled down again. In whispers, I began to apologize for Laura's behaviour.

'She's not normally like this, I don't really know what's got into her . . . maybe it's the new environment, maybe the work is just too hard for her.' I asked him to try to be a bit more patient with her. I understood he no longer wanted a relationship with her, but asked him just to pay her a bit of attention so that she wouldn't feel ignored. He refused to meet my eyes and kept fiddling with his watch strap. I was mortified at finding myself in this position, so soon after declaring my own feelings for him.

It was a few moments before I noticed a strange something in the air. I couldn't place it, but instinct pushed me out of bed again and I rose carefully, unwilling to disturb the others. Oliver followed. We went out into the open air. The night was warm, but there was a distinct smell out here, and in my confusion I thought at first that someone must still be up smoking the herbal stuff. Oliver pointed towards the house. Unusually, there was little moonlight, so it was only possible to make out the bare outline of the chateau against the night sky, and then I heard a kind of crackling sound and suddenly I was running up the steps and I knew the smell was fire and the air was thick with it, and when I neared the top of the steps I could feel the scorching heat on my face and see that the ground floor of one wing was engulfed in flames. Oliver went to wake everyone.

If I had been more alert, if I had moved faster, if I hadn't been so tired that day, if I had known, if I had thought about it, if I had . . . Jesus, I could fill the void with ifs. I started to shout, but my voice drifted meekly into the night and I remembered that the acoustics of the place were such that I had to be actually on the terrace in front of the building to be heard.

One of my duties had been to summon the workers to lunch by ringing the bell in the tower of the disused chapel in one corner of the courtyard, and through the smoke I could see that side was unaffected by flames, so, roaring for help, I shouldered my way through the heavy wooden door and began heaving on the ancient rope until the bell was clanging frantically without rhythm in the chapel tower. The noise of the fire was loud now, cracking, spitting, groaning. I worried that there might be bedrooms directly above the library, which was by now being consumed by a fierce and angry blaze. People began to appear out of the smoke, and all I could glimpse was a scene of chaos, confusion and horror. I found Laura quickly, crying and clinging to an ashen-faced Oliver. I got a few of the lads to drag up the irrigation hoses from the field, but it took ages and when they had unfurled them it became clear they were fixed in position and didn't stretch within ten yards of the fire. Several of the workers to my left were shouting and gesturing, trying to prise open the ancient stone lid of the disused well at the bottom of the terrace steps. Others were dragging a long-abandoned garden hose from the cave-like cellars underneath. Still others stood around staring in shock. Then a creature appeared out of the flames, almost unrecognizable as human, but above the noise of the fire and the roars of instructions, I could hear a high-pitched woman's voice screaming, not in the cut-glass, clean sound one hears from the archetypal heroine on TV, but an ugly, ugly shriek of yearning. I had never heard a sound like that before, and the thought of ever hearing it again fills me with dread. It was the sound of Madame's loss, grief and despair. Her entire body and whatever slight garment she was wearing were blackened, most of her long hair had burned away, and her head was smouldering. I grabbed her and held on tight as she tried to escape me and run into the gaping maw of the inferno, hoarsely screaming all the time 'Papa! Jean-Luc!' until she could scream no longer.

The entire east wing of the house was engulfed in flames which licked and grabbed at falling timbers, tiles and masonry. Later I was to find out that the boy Jean-Luc often used to sleep in a cot bed in his grandad's room on the first floor of that wing. I imagine it was an hour before the fire tenders came from the town, but time means little in the face of the elements; it's an artificial construct that means nothing to the four winds. They pay no heed to ticking clocks. The firemen forced us back and finally took control. They were organized, and I admit that my reaction to their arrival was one of relief, although hope had been long vanquished by the flames.

There was nothing left of the east wing at the end of that night, bar the exterior walls. Through the flame-filled windows, I could only see the night sky and some collapsed roof beams. There was no hope for either of them. Poor Madame – her past and her future utterly wiped out in the unkindest way possible.

It was only after I had deposited Madame into the ambulance, completely broken and still convulsed by silent sobs, that I noticed Oliver was standing behind me, still, silent, his face a mask, his hands shaking as if independent of his wrists. He was in a state of shock.

7. Véronique

Oliver Ryan's name has been in the headlines in the papers here over the last month or two. I have refused to take part in any more media interviews. I cannot help but feel responsible for his attack on his wife. It is tragic, but every time his name is spoken, I automatically think first of the harvest of 1973, and I feel the pain as sharply as I felt it almost forty years ago.

One does not forget the worst time of one's life, no matter how hard one tries. I have spent so many years wishing to change things. What if one had done this, what if one had done that . . . But the ache is still there. Time does not heal. It is a lie. One just gets used to the wound. There is nothing more.

But I must make sense of all this, before it slips through my fingers. One must go back to my father's time to explain everything. One would want everything to be clear.

Papa was made old by *la guerre*, much older than his years. I was a small child at the time of the war, and did not understand anything except that there was a constant stream of visitors to our estate for a certain period. I know now that they were Jewish families protected by my father from the Préfet of Bordeaux in the Vichy regime. It has since been revealed that this civil servant ordered the deportation of 1,690 Jews, including 223 children, from the Bordeaux region to the transit camp at Drancy, near Paris, and then on to death camps in the east.

It is impossible to believe that so many of my compatriots did nothing, but I think genocide happens every day in some part of the world and it is easier for us to pretend that it is not happening, easier to turn off the TV or skip that column in the newspaper.

My father was a hero, an intellectual and a noble man. My mother's death occurred shortly after the occupation, and he was heartbroken, but she had foreseen some of the horror that was to follow and she extracted a promise from my father that he would do everything in his power to protect our friends, no matter what their faith. We lived in very comfortable circumstances in a chateau handed down through seven generations of my father's family. We produced good wines that were sold all over Europe and gave employment throughout the region. My father was less business-orientated than my mother and struggled to keep a rein on things in her absence. He was too distracted and scandalized that the Vichy government could preside over such evil.

He invited several Jewish families to make their homes in the wine cellars underneath the terraced steps, particularly between 1942 and 1944, as the round-ups intensified with the full participation of our own French authorities. Papa refused to stay quiet and made several representations to the secretary general to the Préfecture to no avail. So he took the law into his own hands and, using local informants, was able to pre-empt the official round-ups with round-ups of his own. My Tante Cécile was active in the Resistance movement in the city and, through a network of friends, managed to coordinate the rescue of many families targeted by the Gestapo. The families had to be kept out of sight, and even though we probably had the space for them in the chateau, Papa felt it was too risky. Our chateau was in a valley overlooked on two sides, so it was not possible for any of them to be outside during the daytime. If there was to be a sudden inspection, there must be no trace of them. So Papa set about turning the cellars into a more comfortable home. He knew he risked the business by doing this as wine production would have to cease for the duration. He ordered oil lamps, blankets, books and clothing through some friends in Valence so as not to arouse suspicion in the local village of Clochamps. He took delivery at night and, with trusted friends, created a temporary sanctuary for these families who had nowhere else to run, until a contact could be made to get them north, out of the country and across the border to Switzerland where they were guaranteed to be free of persecution. As a child, it was tremendously exciting for me. A constant stream of new people coming and going. I was too young to notice their sorrow and desperation. Until then, I had been home-schooled, an only child, but Papa made sure that I knew the importance of keeping secrets when it was crucial to do so.

Despite all this activity, my father continued to make time for me, ensuring that I understood the world in a moral sense and that I knew that I would always come first in his life.

In May 1944, just a few months before the Liberation, a midnight raid by the Gestapo found fourteen Jewish families in our cellars, including my best friends Sara and

Marianne. I never saw them again, but was later to discover that they and all their families were dead, some shot while trying to escape the camp at Drancy, others gassed in Auschwitz.

The Gestapo seized our home, had my father arrested by the local police, and I was sent to Tante Cécile in the city. I did not see my father again for six months, but prayed every night for his safe return. I do not remember most of these events and it shames me a little that I do not, but I can visualize the story as it was retold to me by those who were old enough to understand what was happening.

We were reunited for Christmas after the Liberation back at Chateau d'Aigse, but it was barely recognizable as the grand home it had once been. The house had been stripped to its bones; no rugs, paintings, furniture or bedding. Floorboards had been used as firewood. It was the first time I saw my father cry. Whatever they had done to him in prison had broken him. He was just forty-eight years old.

Many years later, I wanted him to get a typewriter and modernize our archaic filing system as it would be easier than filling out the old ledgers we used for the administration of the farm. Papa's refusal was instant and ferocious, and it was only then he told me that while in prison he had been forced to type up deportation orders. He had told nobody and, despite his heroics, he felt nothing but shame. I think it an honourable thing not to visit your horror upon those that you love, but I suspect that the pain of keeping it inside must also cause a lesion to the soul. It was known that when the Gestapo realized they were on the verge of defeat, they became particularly vicious.

I recall the particular warmth of my father holding me tightly in the skeleton of our library, picking over the remnants of our raped bookshelves where he had kept many precious volumes. Papa was a book collector, and I remember that he swore to restore this room first.

Because our winery had ceased production when we were hiding the families (there was no way of operating without the use of the cellars), and my father's nerves were too shattered to return to the business of wine, we had no income apart from what was left of his inheritance. We closed off one wing of the house and confined ourselves to just a few rooms. My privileged childhood was over, but I had no concept of it and so I did not miss it. I was too young to be aware of wealth or the lack of it. I was delighted to attend the local *lycée* as my father tried desperately to nurse his neglected vines back to life. My father begged Tante Cécile to move in with us. He was determined that I should have a mother figure. Tante Cécile was my mother's older spinster sister. The few photographs that remain of my mother show some resemblance, though my mother was beautiful and Cécile was not. She did not know what to do with a child, and we had many battles of will over the most ridiculous things. My father grew weary of being the referee between us, and it took me some time to realize that if Papa trusted her, then I should also trust her. It occurs to me now that they may have been lovers. I have snapshots of catching them awkwardly together in my mind, but no matter. She was a good woman in a difficult situation, and I should have been more aware of the sacrifice she had made to become my guardian.

It was Tante Cécile who spoke to me about how to be a woman and who gave me napkins when menstrual blood first appeared. I thank God for that, because my father was old-fashioned in a lot of ways and could not have countenanced such a conversation, although he proved to be quite the feminist in other ways later on.

I was decidedly average at school but got respectable grades upon graduation. Papa thought it was time for me to go to university in Bordeaux or Paris, but I was not a city girl and could not imagine myself adjusting to life beyond my friends, my father and Cécile. The village girls were not going to university and I thought of myself as one of them. They would mostly end up working on our land in some capacity, so I did not want to mark myself out as different from them. They were good, honest people. Besides, we could not afford three years in the Sorbonne, and I thought that anything I needed to learn, I could learn in Clochamps. I had no ambition to be a doctor or a lawyer, as my father had suggested, and I dreaded telling him this. When I eventually did, his relief was palpable. My father and I had become very close, and he depended upon me more as he aged and his health gradually began to fail.

It was arranged that I would work as secretary to the *maire*, a token job really that took up five half-days a week, although it was rather more demanding to dodge his roaming hands successfully for the ten years I worked there, usually by reminding him loudly of his obligations to his wife and children and by pointing out how very old he was.

I never breathed a word of this to my father. He would

have been horrified, and I was strong enough and confident enough to deal with the old buffoon.

In the afternoons, I returned to my father and Cécile, and helped with the work of maintaining the land and the house as we began a painstaking restoration project.

I had a social life with the other young people in the village, and I attended all the local carnivals and dances, but I did not want a boyfriend. I was sought after by the local boys, and I certainly flirted and exchanged kisses and probably was quite a tease, but I did not fall in love. I cannot understand why, as most of my friends fell in love many times before they married and several times afterwards, but at the back of my mind, I always wondered, *Would Papa like this boy in his house? Would Papa like to see me marry this boy? Could Papa live with this boy?* The answer in my head was always negative. My female friends pitied me, I think, as I attended one wedding after another, assuring me that I would be next, suggesting their cousins and friends as potential partners, but I was happy alone.

The next decade saw the recovery of the vineyard. My father was something of a legendary figure in the entire region. Mostly the villagers felt tremendous guilt that they had done nothing during those terrible years, although we understood their fear. Even known collaborators bent over backwards to help us, and Papa accepted their help graciously, knowing that he was doing them the favour. We drew up plans to restore the house to its former glory, although it was a tediously slow process and, as it later turned out, a futile one.

By the time I was thirty-two, my beloved Tante Cécile had died peacefully in her sleep and my father was bereft again. I, too, felt grief, but whether my father and Cécile were lovers or not, they were certainly confidants and, I suspect, I was often the sole topic of conversation. Cécile thought my father was wrong not to insist that I go to university. She thought I would never meet a suitable husband in our provincial little corner. After she died, Papa began to worry that she was right. It worried him enormously that I was childless. By then, I had had a healthy number of assignations, and had long since lost my virginity to our butcher's nephew Pierre, who came to spend a winter in Clochamps and begged me to marry him at the end of it. It was an intense affair but I saw no future in it, and poor Pierre left the village with a broken heart. Papa had begged me to marry him, or indeed anyone, but I resisted, insisting that I did not want a husband and would never marry. Papa surprised me then by lowering his expectations, suggesting that I take a lover instead. I was shocked, not by the idea of having a lover, which was an entirely acceptable concept, but that my father had suggested it.

'But you need a child!' he pleaded. 'When I am gone, there will be nobody! I am getting old and tired and you are here to care for me, but who will take care of you when you are old? Nobody! Who will take care of this estate?'

I had to concede his point. But looking at the potential gene pool in the village, I could not think of anybody who I would want as a father to my child, except Pierre and he had married and moved north to Limoges.

It had now been six years since my liaison with Pierre. He was strong and handsome and was interested in old maps and books. I began to regret not accepting his proposal, which I think had been sincere. He had not ever met Papa, but they had shared interests, for example books and me, so they might have been friends.

Pierre visited his uncle once a year, and there was the small matter of timing within my cycle to be considered. I know it was deceitful of me, because perhaps I could have told him the truth and got the same result, but I was afraid that Pierre's inherent decency would preclude him from cheating on his wife if I had baldly made my request. All Pierre's qualities were of the kind one would want for one's child, is that not so?

I set out to seduce Pierre, but my window of opportunity was brief as he was only around for two weeks to take lessons from his uncle, the longest-established charcutier in the region, and I had only four or five possible days within that frame to get pregnant.

At first Pierre failed to respond to my seduction, out of fidelity to his wife and concern for my welfare, but I knew he liked me and, although it took some persuasion, thank God he did not make me beg and I did not have to demean myself. The next three nights we spent together in the annexe to his uncle's abattoir. It was not the most auspicious of locations for a seed to be planted, but the breeze through the valley blew the smell of the slaughterhouse downwind, and a little pastis helped us to forget our circumstances. Pierre was a warm and tender lover, and I regretted that this affection was just temporary, that he would be returning to Limoges to his wife. I fell in love a little for the first time. Pierre was terribly sweet and had an innocence about him that I felt I had defiled by the time he left. He was practically apoplectic with apology for leading me astray, and I assured him that we would never speak of it again. I insisted that it would be best if he did not return to the village the following year, and that we both must move on from our folly, and that he must do his best to make it up to his wife. True to his word, Pierre stayed away, and I was glad and sorry.

I was able to confirm my pregnancy, to my father's delight, and in 1967 my precious Jean-Luc was born, a big and healthy baby, to our enormous relief. I realize that having a baby out of wedlock is shameful in some families, and I am sure that the village must have been alive with gossip, but I think that out of respect for my father and me, they started to refer to me as 'the widow'. Better in those days to be a bereaved wife than a single mother. Papa, his mischievous spirit finally returning, was highly amused, as if we had played a successful prank on all our neighbours. 'How is the widow this morning?' he might say, with a wink.

From the time of the birth, Papa and Jean-Luc were inseparable. Papa fashioned a harness out of leather straps and carried Jean-Luc on his back as he went about his business in the markets or at the mayor's office or with the estate manager. As the boy grew, Papa's general mood improved, although he was growing slightly frailer with each passing day. I tried not to be upset when Jean-Luc's first word was *Papi* – Grandpa – particularly since he had been coached from birth to say it. We were completed by him, Papa and I. I had not realized how much I needed my boy until I had him and tried to think of life without him.

In the years that followed, my father returned to his

former self, as if the war had never happened, with renewed vigour and spirit. A peach orchard was planted on one side of the struggling vineyard; an olive grove on the other. Jean-Luc's arrival blessed the house in some way, and our finances began to improve. We began to employ migrant labourers, men and women, to work the land on a seasonal basis. Right up until the summer of 1973.

8. Michael

Nobody slept for days after the fire. Obviously, the vineyard work was cancelled. I proposed going home to Ireland, but Oliver pointed out angrily that it was our duty to stay and help, and Laura agreed. I felt somewhat ashamed. Madame Véronique was discharged from hospital a week later, in time for the funerals. She resembled a ghostly scarecrow, her arms and hands heavily bandaged, her face scorched and what was left of her hair sticking out in tufts. I did my best to make her eat a morsel of this or that, and helped her to apply ointments to her face and head as her skin slowly healed. The kitchens had been largely unaffected by the fire, and I took control of mealtimes for all the people that came to help; but her spirit seemed to have disappeared, as if her body were only carrying the functioning parts she needed for breathing.

Oliver changed on the night of the fire too. Drastically. I knew he had grown close to d'Aigse and the little fellow, but he was grieving as if he were family, seldom talking, his face pinched by sorrow. On the day of the funerals, he disappeared completely, only returning late at night, refusing to answer questions or to be comforted. Laura reckoned that Oliver had replaced his absent father with Monsieur. He undertook to salvage the contents of Monsieur's ruined study – a job he oversaw with great diligence. Laura, already sidelined, was now ignored completely. After two weeks, the bulk of the clearing work was done. There was no question of being paid for our work; we stayed on and got bed and board, the food often donated by neighbouring families and prepared by me. The vineyard was abandoned once again, and there were whispers about the demolition of the east wing. There was nothing more for us to do. We had already missed the first couple of weeks of college. It was time to go. Oliver packed his bags in silence and bade a stoic farewell to Madame, who thanked him for his loyalty and hard work. Some of d'Aigse's map collections had been rescued, though Madame was devastated to lose so many of his books, of which nothing remained but ashes. I remember that Oliver seemed unable to accept the hug of commiseration and left Madame looking awkward and spare. I could have killed him for that, but it was apparent that Oliver was undoubtedly suffering too.

Laura then became a cause for concern once again. Unexpectedly, she refused to come home, insisting that she wanted to stay and help Madame. I couldn't understand what she was thinking; it was just another example of her increasingly erratic behaviour, as far as I was concerned. There were several trunk calls back and forth to Dublin as my parents tried to order her return, but Laura was steadfast. Madame didn't seem to care what happened one way or another, but she assured me that it wasn't a problem if Laura wanted to stay. She could certainly find something for her to do. I had to be satisfied with that. Laura bade us a tearful farewell. She clung to Oliver hopefully, but he was as emotionless and detached as a tombstone.

*

71

The new academic year started slowly, the drab autumn greyness of Dublin seeming so dull compared to the sun-drenched brightness of Bordeaux. I tried to put the trauma of the summer behind me and get back into study and college life. I quickly linked up with some rather camp individuals, the ones I had shunned the previous year out of fear, and began to develop friendships in a different social circle. Even though I still met up with Oliver from time to time, we were clearly estranged, and any time I raised the topic of the summer we had just spent in Bordeaux, he quickly changed the subject, until after a few attempts I never raised it again. I don't know if it was my sexuality, my relationship to Laura or the fact that I reminded him of death that caused the distance between us. Perhaps he blamed Laura for taking us to France in the first place? Whatever was in his head, I needed to move on.

Notwithstanding the harrowing end to my summer, I also returned a different person. Stepping out of the closet was liberating, and there was no way I could go back. My mother got to hear about the company I was keeping and was of course scandalized – threatened to tell my father, call the parish priest; but it was too late. My summer in France had freed me and given me a confidence I never had before. The fire and its devastating consequences made me realize that life was too short to spend any part of it in denial of the truth. I felt at peace in my new skin, almost reborn. I was determined not to be ashamed, despite what the church or the law said.

My mother was trying her level best to get me back into the closet, but I just wasn't having it. Eventually she did tell my father. He was appalled; threatened to disown and disinherit me, and suggested that Laura didn't want to come home because she was ashamed of me. That hurt. I begged for understanding. This is who I am, et cetera, all to no avail. He spoke of the disgrace that I would bring on the family and the humiliation to him personally. I was genuinely sorry for that. I promised him that I would be discreet about my activities, but he was disgusted and ranted about having worked hard all his life only to be confronted with the fact that he had raised a nancy-boy.

In retrospect I must be grateful that my father wasn't a violent man. Lots of fathers were. Dad was hugely disappointed, but it was hard for him and I wonder now if it might not have been better to hide my 'depravity' from my family. Later events would, however, eclipse my coming out and thankfully reunite us as a family, what was left of us.

In November 1973, Father Ignatius was summoned to the house. I didn't know it until he turned up, but I was aware that there was a flurry of cleaning, dusting and vacuuming activity for a week before his arrival. Silver was polished and the 'good' plates and linen tablecloths appeared from wherever they had been quarantined since the previous Christmas Day. I was ushered into our rarely used front room on a Saturday morning, presented to Father Ignatius and left alone with him. I was furious at being tricked into this encounter and I wasn't quite sure what to expect. He wasn't the fire-and-brimstone type – a relatively new appointee to the parish, he was in his early thirties, with a gentle way of speaking. His embarrassment was palpable as, I'm sure, was mine. After some awkward pleasantries, there was a pregnant silence that threatened to give birth any minute. Eventually, I broke its waters by apologizing for having him brought here.

'I suspect that my parents have asked you to come here because I think I'm a homosexual,' I said; and, feeling brazen, added, 'In fact I don't just think it.'

There was a pause, while he coughed unnecessarily and readjusted himself on the leather armchair. It squeaked absurdly as if he had farted, and he quickly and deliberately moved again, causing another squeak, to make it clear that it was the chair and not him. I have eschewed leather furniture ever since.

'It's a sin, you know.'

'I know, Father.'

'Will you swear never to do it again?'

'But, Father, you don't seem to understand. It's not just a matter of *it*, of sexual intercourse, it's a fundamental part of who I am.'

'But it's a sin!'

'I know, Father.'

We went around in circles for a while. I declared that even if I never did *it* again, I wouldn't be able to stop myself from thinking about *it* or indeed the man who might perform *it* with me. He reddened and declared that thinking about it was a sin too and suggested that I could think about flowers or trees instead. I asked him why it was a sin if I wasn't hurting anyone, and he appeared confused.

'What about getting married? Having children?'

'I don't want children.'

'What if you change your mind?'

'About having children or about being gay?'

74

'The first one.'

'What if *you* change *your* mind about having children?'

Silence. He wasn't programmed for that answer.

With another priest, my question to him could have been seen as the height of insolence, but he had a soft way about him and a style that was not intimidating in the least. I felt emboldened.

'I won't,' he said eventually.

'Neither will I.'

'What about the other thing?'

'Being gay? Changing my mind isn't an option! It's not a decision I have made. I have only decided not to hide it any more. Not to hide who I am. I have never been interested in women, as much as I have tried. Don't you think it's unlikely that I might start now?'

'Me neither,' he said.

I thought he had lost the train of our conversation. I wasn't sure what exactly he was agreeing with me about, and then suddenly he buried his head in his hands and broke down, grabbing a handkerchief and stifling his sobs.

I was stunned at this turn of events and found myself consoling him.

'What is it? Look, if I've upset you, I apologize, I never meant . . .'

When he looked up at me imploringly, his long eyelashes glistening wetly, I understood immediately.

'You're not . . . ?' I said. It seemed like it would be blasphemous to even suggest it.

He nodded miserably.

Dermot (his given name) had joined the priesthood in a desperate attempt to escape the reality of his sexuality, as

75

if by ignoring it, he could pretend it wasn't there. The seminary, he later told me, was full of young gay men, most of whom found solace in each other, but he, raised in a more severely Catholic home than my own, was determined not to yield to his inclinations. My confession to him seemed to open the floodgates, and I listened as he recounted his years of utter loneliness, repression and frustration. We talked for three hours. Mum was delighted when we eventually emerged.

The afternoon concluded with my agreeing to meet him for a drink in a small hotel in Bray the following Sunday after Mass. It was clear that Dermot was struggling with the priesthood and with his faith as much as with his sexuality. The church condemned us and yet there were other things going on that the church was ignoring, the full extent of which we have only recently learned. Dermot was aware of some incidents, and had reported them and seen the perpetrators moved or promoted and the 'misdemeanour' covered up. He felt that if he expressed his sexuality it would make him as bad as the abusers, and it took some time for me to convince him that there was a world of difference between two consenting adults engaging in a physical relationship and an older man in a position of power using that power to interfere with a child in some cases not old enough to understand what was being done to them. Dermot went to confession over and over again and spoke to his bishop, tried to be honest with them. They more or less told him to shut up about everything or face a transfer to some godforsaken spot on the globe. After six months of soul-searching, he quit the priesthood altogether and reverted to his given name. We had become close friends and confidants by then, and not long afterwards we became lovers. Before Dermot, I had never thought of settling down with one man. I assumed that, as a gay man, my relationships would probably be fleeting sexual encounters, but I found to my surprise that I loved him deeply and wanted him as a permanent fixture in my life. Thankfully Dermot felt the same way, although it took him a bloody long time to admit it.

But I am skipping ahead. Once I had come out to my parents in the autumn of 1973, I am not sure why I felt the need to, but I wrote to Oliver to tell him officially that I was gay. I think I wanted to explain myself to someone who had known me before and also to excuse the jealousy I felt towards him and Laura that summer. I wanted him to know that he couldn't 'dislike queers' because I was one and I considered him a friend. I think I probably should have been sober when I wrote the letter. I cringe now when I think of it. I received a reply within the week. I don't know exactly what I had wanted or expected, but he admitted that my declaration in the summer was no surprise to him, apologized for trying to set me up with Madame Véronique, wished me well in my life and hoped that I would meet a good man. It seemed clear to me that he was drawing a line under our friendship.

I must have caused quite a degree of stress for my parents around that time. There were more trials and tribulations when I declared my intention to drop out of college and open a restaurant. This time, though, Mum was on my side and eventually convinced my father to lend me the capital required. I had practically moved into the kitchen in the months after my return from France, and Mum was delighted at all my discoveries. Some ingredients I had brought home with me and some I imported from my deflorist Thierry. Dad was impressed by the food but thought I should be spending more time with my books, although when I single-handedly did the catering for a dinner party they were hosting for twelve of their most sophisticated friends, who swooned over each course, my father was persuaded to concede that I had a gift worth investing in.

All these negotiations served to distract us from the fact that Laura had stated that she wasn't coming home for Christmas. Her irregular letters home told of the building project undertaken to restore the east wing as a result of donations from all over the province. Though somewhat mystified, we were proud of Laura's charitable actions and despatched a large hamper accompanied by an equally large bank draft courtesy of my father.

My restaurant, L'Étoile Bleue, opened at the end of March 1974 in a laneway off a Georgian square in the city centre. In the space of a year, my life had turned upside down in spectacular style. The restaurant did good business from the start, and within a few months I could see that if trade continued at the current rate, I would be able to repay my father's investment within maybe five or six years, so all was fabulous. Then, in August, Laura came home.

My parents were, of course, relieved and I wanted to hear all about what was happening in Clochamps, how the building project was going in Chateau d'Aigse, how Madame Véronique was, whether she had seen Thierry, and so on. Laura answered my questions but seemed distant and uninterested. She looked pretty dreadful too: she had dark circles under her eyes and she was very thin. She just picked at her food at mealtimes. We didn't recognize her odd behaviour for the nervous breakdown she was having. My mother brought her to a doctor who recommended a foul-smelling tonic that had no effect whatsoever. When I suggested getting in touch with Oliver, she barely reacted at all. I didn't understand what was going on with Laura, but I was worried. I offered her a few weeks' work in the restaurant. She had deferred college for a year and still had more than a month before she started again. She would be OK for a few days and then she wouldn't show up at all, leaving us frustrated and short-staffed. She said she was tired. 'Of what?' I said. 'You don't bloody do anything!'

Reluctantly I approached Oliver to ask if he would call to the house to see her. He obliged by offering to take her out for a meal in my restaurant or anywhere she wanted, but Laura refused to go. Oliver even wrote her a letter, but Laura didn't want to see him. I wondered if perhaps there was more to Oliver and Laura's break-up than I knew. To all outward appearances, he had been a gentleman through-out their entire relationship – there was no question that he had cheated on her or anything like that – but it was clear that Laura wasn't going to forgive him for rejecting her. Usually it was Laura who did the rejecting. She clearly couldn't handle being on the receiving end. I didn't think that Oliver could be held responsible for her depression. Not then.

9. Stanley

I find it difficult to believe what is being said and written about Oliver. It is true that I haven't seen him in decades, but the person they are describing in the headlines is not the boy I knew.

When Oliver became so hugely successful as Vincent Dax, I was really glad that his life had worked out so well, because as far as I remember he had a fairly miserable childhood, even by Irish standards. I know because I was there for part of it. They say that children always accept their own reality as normality, so I suspect that Oliver wasn't that aware of how neglected he was, but it was certainly whispered about at the time.

My father had died the year before I arrived in St Finian's in south Dublin. I was fourteen and had three sisters. I think Mammy just wanted me to have a more stable education and to have some masculine influences on my life. We lived in rural south Kilkenny and I ended up working the farm quite a bit, but Mammy was determined that I wouldn't follow my father into an early grave, which, she insisted, was a result of working his fingers to the bone from dawn till dusk. The other more pressing reason, though I didn't appreciate it at the time, was my chronic shyness. I have a disfiguring port wine stain across my left eye and for most of my life have been self-conscious about it. My mother felt that if she didn't find a way to get me off the farm at a young age, I would probably never leave home. She was right.

St Finian's wasn't a bad school by the standards of the day. I don't ever remember there being reports of sexual abuse or anything like that. The priests were, by and large, quite kind. There was the token sadist, naturally enough, but I reckon having only one on staff in an entire school in the 1960s was a pretty good ratio.

When I arrived in Oliver's class, he had already been in St Finian's for eight years. It seems really shocking now; the thought of sending my own little fella away when he was only six sends shivers down my spine, but it really wasn't that unusual at the time. Oliver was pretty quiet, most notable for the fact that his clothes were almost threadbare. Because of this and because of his dark complexion, he was an obvious target for general slagging. Academically, he was pretty average, better at French than anything else though still not outstanding. For the first year, before I really got to know him, I assumed he was a scholarship child because he seemed so, well . . . poor. We knew he had no mother and assumed that she was dead. It was rumoured that Oliver's dad hadn't been married to Oliver's mother or that she might have died in childbirth. He never spoke of her and it was just one of those things that was understood; it would be inappropriate to ask, like the fact that we all knew Simon Wallace was adopted but no one ever mentioned it.

Oliver spoke of his father though, often, and with reverence and pride. I can't remember exactly what it was he did, something to do with the church, senior adviser to the Archbishop of Dublin, something like that. It was surprising to me that Oliver's dad would be someone of importance because his general neglect of, and lack of interest in, his own son was staggering. What shocked me even more was the fact that Oliver had a sibling, a pale-eyed blond-haired half-brother, Philip, about seven years younger than him, who lived at home and went to the primary school attached to our school. I never saw them speak to each other in intimate terms. It was as if they were completely unrelated. But the most awful thing was that Oliver's home was less than a mile from the school and he seemed to be forbidden from entering it. At Christmas time and during school holidays, Oliver stayed with the priests. From the window of the corridor beside the science laboratory on the top floor of the school, you could see Oliver's house. Many, many times, I found him perched on the windowsill, often with my pair of binoculars, watching his family come and go. Somehow, it seems much more tragic now. In the macho world of an all-boys' boarding school, there was no room for sentimentality or sympathy. If we were wounded, we learned to hide it well.

Oliver and I became friends in my second year at the school in a passive kind of way. We didn't exactly choose each other. It was just because everyone else had friends and we were the two oddities with whom no one else wanted to hang out. My disfigurement and Oliver's manifest neglect marked us as outsiders. He named us 'The Weirdos'. We didn't belong in the hip crowd and we didn't belong in what we called the 'mumsy' crowd, and as we weren't part of any particular gang, we buffeted along between all the various groups, falling out of favour with one and moving on to the next. I believe we trusted each other. Oliver dominated the friendship, which really suited me fine. I pretty much went along with anything he said, but he wasn't much of a rule-breaker or risk-taker so I was never led into jeopardy. He never mentioned my eye and I never mentioned his mother. That was the basis of a firm friendship in those days.

He was curious about my family, constantly asking me to retell stories and anecdotes from my holidays at home. Not having a mother, he wanted to know about mine.

Oliver's father visited maybe once every year or eighteen months. Oliver would be in a knot of anxiety for weeks leading up to a visit, trying his best to raise his grades and keep out of any hint of trouble. He looked forward to it and dreaded it in equal measure, I think. When my mother or other parents visited, they always brought gifts for their children, usually a tuck box of some description or, if you had particularly cool parents, a set of darts, water pistols or other weapons of minor destruction.

A boy would always be very popular in the wake of a parental visit as he would be expected to share the swag. Some suggested that Oliver was keeping it for himself and simply refused to share, but I know that wasn't the case. His father never brought him anything, except a book of psalms once.

Approaching summer holidays towards the end of my second year there, my mother suggested that I invite Oliver to join us on the farm for a few weeks. I wasn't sure about this plan, if I'm honest. It was one thing to be hanging out in school, whittling catapults out of branches and spying on the school nurse and her boyfriend, Father James, but school and home were very different environments. My home was a particularly feminine one, with a widowed mother and three girls, while Oliver was growing up in a school surrounded almost exclusively by men, except for the aforementioned nurse and a few of the jolly cleaners. I remember being worried by his reaction to my family and vice versa, but I needn't have. All the women in my family fell in love with him. My mother would have adopted him if she could, and it was the most painful embarrassment to watch all my sisters going through the various stages of romantic attraction to him. Una, the youngest, was nine and spent as much time as possible climbing on to him for piggybacks or asking him to read to her. Michelle, thirteen, feigned a sudden curiosity in anything that Oliver had an interest in and spent her time baking new delicacies with which to charm him. Aoife, at sixteen, one year older than us, tried a different tack, pretending that she didn't notice him, but always seemed to be in some state of undress when we walked in from the barn and developed a way of draping herself over our furniture that could only be described as louche.

Oliver took it in his stride. I'm sure he was somewhat discomfited, but he must have been flattered all the same. That was probably the first time he'd been around women of his own age. At first he was shy and overly polite, but he gradually relaxed until he almost became accepted as one of the clan. The plan was that he would stay three weeks. His father had apparently stipulated that Oliver must earn his keep and be put to work on the farm, but we were all used to working our summers on the farm anyway, so Oliver blended in quite well. Oliver proudly sent his first postcard to his father, telling him how much he was enjoying his time and assuring him that he was working hard none-theless. Two days later, my mother received a phone call from Mr Ryan instructing her to return Oliver to the school immediately. He should have had another eight days with us, but Oliver's father would brook no argument and offered no reason for the change of plan. My mother was very upset, I recall, and bought Oliver a whole new set of clothing before we put him on the train back to Dublin. Oliver bade us farewell stoically. He didn't question his father's decision or express resentment. He didn't seem angry about it, but I clearly remember the shine of tears in his eyes as we waved him goodbye from the station plat-form, my three sisters blowing him kisses, my mother as heartbroken as they were.

We never got a valid reason for Oliver's sudden depart-ure. As far as I know, he just went back to the school and spent the rest of the summer with the priests. My mother always maintained that his father acted out of spite, that the postcard alerted him to the fact that Oliver might actu-ally be enjoying himself and so he felt compelled to put a stop to it. There wasn't really any other explanation, I'm afraid. It is hard to credit that anyone could be so cruel to their own flesh and blood. I guess we will never know the reasons why, unless Oliver writes his autobiography. But I'm not sure if he would be allowed to do that now.

When we left school, Oliver went to college and I returned to the farm. We would meet up occasionally in Dublin for a few drinks. I knew from rumours that he had a small flat in Rathmines and worked mornings and weekends in a fruit and vegetable market to pay his rent. I guess once he was educated, his father washed his hands of him, his duty done. Oliver spent summers working abroad to pay his college tuition, and I think he must have flourished and gained confidence during that time. One summer he went with a gang from college to work on a vineyard. Apparently there was some tragedy connected with a fire, but I never heard the full story as we lost contact around that time.

In December 1982, I was pleased to receive an invitation to Oliver's wedding to a girl called Alice who was illustrating a book he had written. I was happy that he had found both love and a publisher. My mother was ill in hospital at the time, and I couldn't make it to the wedding. It was a shame. I would have liked to have celebrated his happy day with him.

Just a few months later, I got an invite to the launch of Oliver's first book. I was confused at first as the author's name on the invite was Vincent Dax, but when I rang to query it, the publisher let me know that it was Oliver.

There were only ten or twelve people there; one was Father Daniel from the school, two or three were his friends from college who I had come across once or twice, and of course his agent, publishing folk, and his new bride, Alice. She was lovely, very warm and gracious. I recall that even though she had illustrated the book, she insisted that it was Oliver's night and Oliver's success.

Oliver was a nervous wreck and immediately I recognized why. He was waiting for his father. The fearful boy so desperate to impress that I recalled from schooldays hadn't completely disappeared yet. All evening, as people congratulated him and he read passages from the book,

Oliver's eyes swivelled backwards and forwards to the door. I asked him eventually if his father was expected. He gave me a look that said it was none of my business and not up for discussion. Later we had a few drinks in Neary's and he relaxed a bit. I asked him why he had used a pseudonym. He grew embarrassed, and I guessed that perhaps his father had insisted upon it.

Since then, I have only seen Oliver a handful of times, but I noticed that when I met him, he seemed increasingly casual and breezy in conversation and almost dismissive of our shared childhood. Finally, he stopped returning my calls and didn't respond to invitations.

He popped up on TV sometimes on the review programme or as a pundit on the radio, but it is years since we really knew each other socially.

When I grew up and met Sheila and we had our little boy Charlie, I often thought about what fatherhood should be. My own father had killed himself with work and was barely a presence in our lives; Sheila's father was the local GP in Inistioge and by all accounts cared more for his community than his family. Other fathers may be violent alcoholics or too idle to provide for their own. None of us are perfect. I did my best with Charlie, and he is now a fine young man who makes me proud every day. Some men, though, they shouldn't be fathers; they are not cut out for it.

10. Oliver

My earliest memories are confused. A dark room in a Gothic house. I was alone for most of the day, but sometimes an old lady gave me food and was kind. Her name, I think, was Fleur, or perhaps that is just a name I gave her. I remember being told that I must keep myself tidy because my father was coming up to see me, but I accidentally spilled some red juice on my shirt and I wasn't allowed to see him as a result. Fleur was French, and I think I may have spoken French before I spoke English. She taught me to read a little in both languages. She hugged me sometimes, and called me her *pauvre petit cœur*. I recall my father came to my room one time and Fleur was nervous. He stared at me and then roughly pulled at me, examining my hair, my teeth. What was he looking for? I cried then, and he shouted at the woman and left the room, slamming the door behind him.

Fleur told me that my father was getting married to a lady called Judith. I saw her once from the top of the stairs. She was beautiful and very fair. I remember wishing that I could be blond like her. She did not see me and I never spoke to her. I was not allowed to attend the wedding.

My next memory is of Fleur packing a suitcase for me, and she was pretending to be happy but her eyes were wet. She told me that I was going on a great adventure and that I would have lots of playmates. I was excited, but at the gates of the boarding school I realized that she was not coming with me, and I grabbed her legs and begged her not to leave me there, but a gentle priest lifted me in his arms and distracted me with a toy truck, and when I turned to show it to Fleur, she was gone.

I was one of the youngest boys in the school, but I settled in well. I was not used to much attention and was mesmerized by the constant bustle of activity. I was not so homesick as the other boys, because, as I now know, one is not sick for home, but for the people in it. I pined a little for Fleur, but not too much. I was not the most popular boy and I was not at the top of the class, but I tried my hardest. I heard from other boys about living with mothers and fathers and siblings, and I came to understand that fathers were often stern and that the only way to appease them was to get good report cards.

But regardless of how hard I studied and how good my report card was, I failed to win my father's approval.

I was not permitted to go home during the holidays and rattled around with the priests for the summer months. Every other year, my father would visit and the priests and I would scrub up in preparation. They were as in awe of him as I was, because it was a diocesan school and my father was in control of the finances. The school depended upon his decisions for funding. I would sit on one side of the headmaster's desk, and my father would stand behind me, refusing to sit or take tea. I would be as still as I could, but could not stop my hands from buttoning and unbuttoning my shirt cuffs. Father Daniel would tell him that I was doing well, even when I wasn't. My father would ask to inspect my report cards and enquire about my general health and then he would leave, without touching me or looking in my direction. Father Daniel was embarrassed for me and would try to make a joke of my father's distance.

'Isn't he a busy fella, your dad? Eh?'

It was Father Daniel who told me that I had a younger brother, Philip, born a year after my father and Judith wed. He is blond like his mother. He joined the primary school as a day pupil when I was in the senior boarding school. I watched him grow up in a way, because I could see my father's house from a window on the top corridor and I had an almost permanent loan of Stanley's binoculars, with which I spied on my father's new family. I watched my brother come and go from my father's house; watched Judith pottering in the garden; watched them all out in the driveway, admiring my father's new car together. I envied Judith and Philip.

School sports days were a particular kind of torture. In the first few years, when I thought my father might actually turn up, I tried my hardest in the weeks leading up to the event, rising early and doing extra training. If my father would not acknowledge my academic achievement, I thought perhaps he might be impressed by my athletic prowess. In the early days I won medals and trophies every year, but my father never appeared.

The other boys' families would descend upon the school, the mothers dolled up and reeking of perfume so strong that it would make your eyes water, accompanied by the fathers in their highly polished cars. There would be sulking or boisterous siblings, and small babies swaddled in pastel shades and shrieking and tantrums. Significantly, there would be a great deal of hugging and affectionate ruffling of hair and manly handshakes. And after the sporting events, there would be a grand picnic on the lawns, where the families would sit together in huddled groups. Father Daniel did his best to distract me from my isolation on these days, employing me in tasks of 'great importance'. Even when I did not win a medal, he would single me out for special mention.

I never gave up hope that my father might one day remember me. In my fantasy, he suddenly realized that he was wrong about me and that I was not a bad boy. He would come to the school and take me home to live with him and tell me that I was a wonderful son.

And then in my penultimate year at St Finian's, I was overjoyed finally to see my father arrive in a black Mercedes with Judith by his side. They could have walked, but I think the car was a status symbol that needed to be displayed. They parked up in the lower car park and I ran down the lane towards the car, my heart pounding, barely hoping that my fantasy might become reality. My joy turned to bitter dismay when I saw Philip climb out of the car behind them and I remembered that my father was there for him, for Philip. My pace slowed and I stopped in the middle of the lane and did not know whether to turn back or not, but it was too late. My father looked up and saw me. He nodded quickly at me and raised his hand, and I thought for a moment that he was summoning me, but in the same instant he looked over at Judith, who just looked startled, and what could have been a wave of acknowledgement revealed itself to be a gesture of dismissal and I knew I was not welcome in their company. For the rest of the day, I feigned illness and retired to the infirmary until the festivities were over.

The following year, I did not enter any event, pleading exam pressure. I stayed in the study hall for the entire day, trying to block out the sound of the tannoy, the cheering and the laughter. Stanley came in later with a cake his mother had baked especially for me. A giddiness overtook me and I indulged in a food fight with him, tearing the cake apart and flinging fistfuls of jam and sponge at him, at the walls, at the light fittings and the portraits of former masters. We laughed until our sides were sore, but our glee was different. Mine was bordering on hysteria.

Stanley was a friend, a real friend back then. I knew that I was different from the other children by the time I was in the senior school. They talked of holidays and cousins and fights with their sisters and Christmas presents and politics at the family dinner table. I had nothing to offer in these conversations. I was also marked out by my obvious lack of money. My uniforms came from the school's lost-and-found office, and I had no money for the tuck shop. There was an unspoken agreement that Father Daniel would provide whatever I needed. I do not know if this was instigated by my father or if it was a simple act of kindness on Father Daniel's part. I suspect the latter. But a teenage boy often has more wants than needs, and I could not ask Father Daniel for stink bombs or plastic catapults or gobstoppers or dirty magazines.

Stanley Connolly shared all these things with me and, indeed, Stanley gave me my first glimpse of home life when I went to stay with his family on their farm in Kilkenny. I was surrounded by women for the first time. Stanley's mother was a widow and he had three sisters. They terrified me. I had hit puberty and was barely in control of my hormones. I was tall and strong for my age and well able to do the farm work, but in the evenings when the family would gather for dinner, the noise and chattering of the girls unnerved me. I felt somewhat as if I had been mistakenly locked into a cage of exotic animals in the zoo.

They were incredibly kind and generous to me, and I know now that the girls were openly flirting with me. I should have been delighted with the attention, but I felt that the devotion was unwarranted, that any minute they would discover that I was a fraud, that they would realize a boy who did not deserve a mother could not belong in a family, blessed among women. I imagined that, like some unfamiliar species, they might all turn on me. Kill me. Eat me. I do not like cats for the same reason.

Stanley's mother constantly fussed over me. She wanted to know what my favourite food was, and my uncultured palate betrayed me because I really only knew meals by the days of the week. Mondays: bacon and cabbage; Tuesdays: sausages and mashed potato; and so on. Eating real butter, home-baked bread and fresh meat and vegetables on unscheduled days made me uncomfortable. In school, we had fish on Fridays and that was my preference. 'What kind of fish?' she asked, and I could not tell her, but said that it was white, triangular-shaped and usually about four inches long. Mrs Connolly laughed, but I could see that she was sad for me, and from then on she set about awakening my taste buds, which, while sweet and generous, only made me uneasier. I knew my manners and ate everything that was served, but my stomach was so unused to such richness that sometimes, at night, cramps would keep me awake until the small hours. On one of those nights, I resolved that I would learn about food when I was properly grown up and that I would not be embarrassed again.

I did not realize the extent of my institutionalization, but I was self-conscious about being the object of their pity, or admiration, or whatever it was, and when my father ordered me to leave, I was almost relieved to do so. Stanley was a witness to my poverty and my isolation, and I think he knew more about my circumstances than I told him. This embarrassed me, so I did not make much of an effort to keep in touch with him when I left that school, not until I got married and had my first success with a book and had the proof that I was not a failure, but by then years had passed and we had little in common beyond the memory of shared catapults.

Many years ago, I went into town for a meeting with a publicist and I was early. It was a beautiful, warm summer's day, and I decided to take a walk through St Stephen's Green. As I passed the children's playground, I saw Stanley pushing a little boy on a swing. The likeness was extraordinary, though the little boy was not cursed with the facial discolouration of his father. Stanley was older now and there were flecks of grey in his hair, which he still wore in a long fringe in a futile attempt to cover the mark.

Stanley could not take his eyes off his son, as if he could not believe his luck. He and the boy were in their own world, oblivious to this strange man watching. The boy threw his head back and laughed a hearty cackle as he swung ever higher, and I wanted to be him more than anybody else in the world. Just for a moment, to exult in a father's love and attention. Then the boy stopped the swing, scuffing his little sandals into the gravel to apply the brakes. He jumped off and ran to a red-haired lady sitting on a bench nearby. Her lipsticked mouth grinned at the boy and she scooped him up into her arms and he buried his face into the soft slope of her neck. I felt only envy.

I heard a loud cough right behind me, and when I turned to see a park-keeper in a soiled uniform glaring at me, I realized how it must appear – an adult solo male mesmerized by the children's playground. We both thought of each other as a sick bastard and, incensed, I left immediately, stopping for a swift Jameson in Peter's Pub to steady my cuff-buttoning hands before my meeting.

Perhaps I should have had children with Alice, but I knew that any child would only remind me of a small French boy so full of charm and mischief, and long dead. I might even have been a father figure to Alice's brother Eugene, but something told me that if my father had so strongly disapproved of me, a strong and handsome and successful young man, then Eugene, an overweight mental defective, would have appalled him.

11. Eugene

St Catherine's House

PATIENT NO: 114

ANNUAL REPORT: 17/12/1987

NAME: Eugene O'Reilly

DATE OF ADMISSION: 22/07/1987

DOB: 17/05/59

HEIGHT: 5 foot 8 inches

WEIGHT: 16 stone 9 lbs

HAIR: Brown

EYES: Blue

MENTAL CAPACITY: Eugene is of limited intellect with an estimated mental age of seven or eight years. He can't read or write, although he likes to have books in his possession, and needs help dressing himself (buttons, laces). He can feed himself, although he must be watched at mealtimes as he will not stop eating until food is removed from him. Most of the time he can perform his toilet tasks without assistance. He has little interest in television but loves music, although his physical reaction to music can be upsetting to other residents. Eugene is unaware of his own strength and size.

HISTORY: Eugene O'Reilly was admitted in July of this year by his brother-in-law Oliver Ryan (the author Vincent Dax). Eugene was in good general health, although Nurse Marion reported some bruising to the upper arms and body. These marks were explained by Mr Ryan, who said that Eugene had often to be restrained after episodes of aggression. Mr Ryan very much regretted the incidents that led to these bruises but suggested that he had little choice in the matter, as Eugene was not capable of controlling his temper. Mr Ryan reported that Eugene had become violent and difficult since the death of Eugene's mother in 1986 and that he could no longer be cared for in the family home, particularly in the light of a recent arson attempt that Mr Ryan insists was malicious. It was notable that there seemed to be some difference of opinion on this issue between Mr Ryan and his wife, the patient's sister Alice Ryan. Mr Ryan maintains that his wife is unrealistic about Eugene's abilities and propensity to violent outbursts.

ASSESSMENT: In adults with the type of moderate to severe learning difficulties Eugene presents, violence and aggression are unusual, but clearly Mr Ryan was correct in his assessment of Eugene, as he has displayed extreme aggression in his objection to being left in our care, and unfortunately two of our porters were required to take Eugene to the lockdown unit after Mr Ryan left. Eugene has had

great difficulty settling into
St Catherine's and has caused major
disruption among other residents. In
particular, he attempts to pick up other
residents while they are seated, running
the length of corridors, holding them
high above his head within their chairs.
While this may be a source of amusement
to some residents, to others it is
terrifying and we cannot allow the health
and safety of any of our patients to be
jeopardized. Eugene has been reprimanded
for this activity on several occasions
and has reacted belligerently when
physically restrained. Although we are
reluctant to medicate Eugene to subdue
his boisterous nature, it has become our
only option.

Eugene is highly verbal at times, and at
other times almost totally silent.
Mr Ryan warned us that Eugene could not
be depended upon for veracity, and indeed
we have found that Eugene seems often to
inhabit a world of fantasy in which he
imagines that he is a prince of a magical
kingdom. Through trial and error, we have
learned that it is best to leave Eugene
to his own devices.

In his first two months here, Eugene's
sister visited him almost every day, but
her visible upset at leaving Eugene
communicated itself to him and I took the
decision to write to Mr Ryan to ask him
to confine his wife's visits to just once
a week. Mrs Ryan cannot be dissuaded
from bringing with her home-baked
cakes and confectionery, which I think

best to confiscate for the good of Eugene's health.

Noreen McNally

Executive Director of St Catherine's Residential Care Facility

My mammy loved me and Alice loved me and Barney loved me and God loved me I said my prayers every night every night I still say my prayers and I ask God to bless Mammy in heaven and Alice and my friend Barney but sometimes I forget sometimes I forget. I remember I remember Barney is my friend he used to take me for a drive in his car his ears stick out like a clown hahaha he makes me laugh and tickles me and tells me stories and brings me flying he is Grimace and I am Prince Sparkle and he helps me battle with the evil Queen who does wee-wees in her knickers hahaha.

Oliver? No nonononono. Oliver is the baddy man he stealed Alice from me and Mammy and Barney where is Mammy I want Mammy Oliver hurted me he pinched my arm and squeezed and squeezed I had a big purple bruise Alice is coming she brings me cakes and reads stories she says Oliver made Prince Sparkle she says Oliver writed it down but I know he didn't he didn't he didn't Oliver is the bad Queen dressed up as a man.

Where is Barney? I miss Barney where is my Mammy I remember now she's dead in a box in the mud she doesn't like it to be dirty I don't want to be dead why are all the dead people in the mud my daddy is in the mud too but I seed him in photos and Alice telled me he was a great man.

I forget lots of things all the time but I remember being in my house with Mammy and Alice and Barney visiting and telling me stories. Barney told me he was going to marry Alice and I could live with them but it's a secret and I'm not telling anyone I wish he would hurry up because Oliver the baddy man already married Alice and it's Barney's turn now. Alice went away when Oliver married her and they lived in a flat I visited two times but I was only allowed in Alice's corner and Oliver has a locked-up green box for his writing and me and Alice are not allowed to see in the box. I want to know what's in the box but Alice says it's Oliver's private business. One time I was looking at the box and Oliver shouted at me just for looking I think there's a monster in the box. I wasn't allowed to visit Alice after that and I was sad but Barney came and read me stories and we went in his car I'm not allowed in the front seat because I can't stop beeping the horn Barney thinks it's funny but the baddy men in the other cars are very cross very cross and I have to sit in the back. Mammy got sick and was in the hospital. Mammy is dead. After Mammy went in the mud Alice came home to live and that was nice I miss Mammy where is Mammy oh yes dead in the mud. Oliver came to live in our house too he is mean and calls me bad names and it's my house and Alice's house not Oliver's house. I hate Oliver he punched me when Alice wasn't looking and then he telled a lie he calls me a big fat pig I am big and fat but a man he is a pig stealing Alice and Mammy's house he said I had to have my dinner in the kitchen and it's his house now and he's the boss of me but I like the kitchen and I like Mammy's and Alice's and my house but not when Oliver is the boss. Oliver took my flying chair and goned it somewhere I don't know Barney doesn't come and do flying any more now he can't no chair. Oliver fell over in the garden one time and I laughed and laughed it was funny. He went to the hospital and when Alice came home, Oliver told her that I hurted him his tail is as long as a telephone wire but he locked me in my room and I shouted all night until Alice let me out she was crying and it wasn't funny any more and I was sorry for laughing when Oliver hurted himself. Then another time I was sitting at Alice's dressing table brushing my hair with her silver hairbrush that was Mammy's she's in the mud and Oliver came in and smashed the mirror and turned the dressing table upside down. I was frightened and Alice came running and the big fat liar says I done it but I didn't for cross my heart and hope to die and then it's my birthday and I have a cake with birthday candles and I blow them out and wish that Oliver isn't here but Oliver is nice to me on my birthday and lets me play with his lighter that is shaped like an aeroplane in the shed in the garden but there is an accident and I am very bad boy because I started a fire and help! help! like in *Jane Eyre* one of Alice's favourite books. Oliver says he is scared of me and doesn't want to be in the house with me hurrah this makes me happy and dancing because Oliver is going away but he isn't going away I am going away and I hate him.

Oliver said I had to come and live here in St Catherine's I don't know what St Catherine's is I think it's where a saint lives and I said yes if Alice comes too. He lied and said Alice was coming too Alice told a big fat lie and then she is crying crying and it's me making her sad and Oliver says it's me making her sad I have to go to St Catherine's on my own. No Mammy.

I was frightened here in the start where is Saint Catherine not here no saints here just some mad people I know I'm a bit mad Barney told me I'm a bit mad in a good way but the people who live here are really mad in a mad way much more mad than me and some of them shouting but not in words just in noises I don't like shouting and some of them like dead people strapped in wheelchairs and fed like babies with bibs and televisions on everywhere loud louder.

And the boss is a lady Miss Noreen who is all smiley and laughing when she rings Oliver to tell him I've been a bad boy I can hear her through the wall in the nurses' station but here no smiles laughs chats but Lord Snooty face and ignoring everyone only shouting at the nurses where is Mammy I remember now in the mud where is Alice she used to come on Tuesdays with cakes and we play games only now she doesn't come any more either. In the start I was really scared and want to go home to my own room and my own bed with my record player that Barney gave me but Alice says I live with twelve friends some of them don't like me and some of them love me Nurse Marion is my favourite I don't like Miss Noreen makes me sit with my hands under my legs Christy is very old he dribbles like I used to Mammy said that was bad manners and I told Christy but he was shouting and Miss Noreen said go to your room it's not my room it's all of our room there's Christy, Billy, Malachy, Conal and I forget the others we share a big room and no talking when lights are out and no stories at bedtime and no jam sandwiches in bed I remember Barney jam sandwiches and stories with the Selfish Giant and the one about Alice going down the hole with the rabbit but I'm in a story with Grimace and I am the Prince so that's my favourite one Christy went in the mud yesterday no more dribbling thank God.

He was dead in his bed and I told him look after Mammy in the mud Nurse Marion is my favourite one she's here in the daytime and gives me sweets our secret Alice didn't come yesterday, or last week, or lots of weeks. I seed Miss Noreen and Nurse Marion fighting. Miss Noreen made Nurse Marion cry Nurse Marion asked me about Barney and where he lives I telled Nurse Marion that Barney is my friend and she ringed him up and now he is visiting me every day he telled me that Alice is in Happyland drawing pictures and flying around in a chair. She is not in the mud. He sweared me that and Barney always telled the truth. Barney says we can visit Alice when I am growed up, but I think I am a growed-up. Barney says I must be growed up more.

12. Oliver

My study is a high-ceilinged room at the rear corner on the left-hand side of the house. When Alice's father was alive, he might have used it as an office or a den, but when we moved in, it was a kind of playroom for Eugene. Full of soft toys, picture books and an old record player, it was grubby and disorganized. In the centre of the room, on an old, foul-smelling rug, there was a chair that might have been more suited to the kitchen – Shaker-style, with spokes emanating from the seat to a bar across a low back, and arm rests. It had been painted many times over the years, and several layers of blue, red and yellow paint flaked under the general grime. This apparently was Eugene's 'flying chair'. I suppose I should have been flattered that my first book inspired the flying chair, but it certainly was not what I had in mind.

The room was bright and airy, however, with two tall sash windows dominating the two exterior walls, one looking out to the back lawn, the other on to the side path of the house. The two interior walls were decorated in floral wallpaper, punctuated here and there with Disney posters, Duran Duran wall charts and Michael Jackson album covers.

It was the only room in the house with a sturdy brass lock on the door, and I insisted that this was the only room in which I would be able to write. Alice was at first reluctant, but I persuaded her that we could fit out a room upstairs for Eugene – in what would have been her old bedroom (we had moved into her parents' bedroom). One day, when she and Eugene went out for the afternoon, I stripped the room bare, gutting it, and dragged all the detritus on to a bonfire at the end of the garden. The fuss that ensued was unwarranted, in my opinion. Eugene was most upset about the damn chair. As if the house were not full of chairs, all of them better than that particular specimen. He sobbed like a baby, and I realized quickly that I could not live with this kind of disturbance.

I redecorated the room to my own taste. A gentleman's room, with teak panelling and bookcases lining the interior walls, and heavy velvet curtains framing the windows. I had the long-disused fireplace opened up, and I placed my antique mahogany partner's desk at an angle facing the two windows. At an auction, I later purchased a leather upholstered library chair, a standard lamp to be placed behind my chair, and also a desk lamp with a green glass shade. Subtle lighting is very important. From a company in the UK, I purchased a leather-bound desk blotter, and, from a vintage bookseller, a few select first editions with which to fill my bookcases. Within a few short weeks, the room looked like a writer's room, and indeed, on the few occasions when I have granted interviews at home, the interrogator has in every instance remarked on how atmospheric the room is, exactly how they imagined the study of an award-winning author. As if, just by getting the look right, the words would flow.

Alice knew that I must not be disturbed. It pleases me that she thought my genius required isolation and silence.

I used it to good effect when that little moron Eugene wanted to know what was in the green wooden box. Alice never showed much curiosity, but Eugene would not give up. He was obsessed by it. On the few occasions that I allowed Eugene and Alice into the room, he would waddle over to the bookcase and look up to the top shelf, where I had placed it.

'What's in the box, Oliver? What's in the box? Is there a monster in the box, Oliver? What's in the box?'

'Nothing,' I would insist, 'just boring birth certificates, passports and insurance documents. Nothing to interest you.'

'Show me! Show me! I want to see what's in the box! Show me what's in the box!', stamping his foot for emphasis, and I would call Alice and complain that he was disturbing me, and demand that she remove him from my presence. He would often hover outside the door, waiting for me to come out, and as soon as I opened it, he would dart in on top of me. 'What's in the box, Oliver?'

Eventually I informed Alice that I could no longer write while Eugene lived under our roof. She agreed finally to his moving out when I found an obliging care home willing to take him. It was not cheap, a fact that Alice seemed not to appreciate. She accused me of 'hating' him. She overestimated my feelings for her brother: I simply did not want him around.

Alice continued to whinge for years, used to bring him out to the house at Christmas time for the first couple of years, but every single time it reopened the arguments and I felt it was in everybody's best interests just to put a stop to it. The last Christmas that he came, I got him alone in the kitchen and told him a very special story in words that he could understand, and made it very clear that he would be unwise ever to visit again. Afterwards, he just walked up and down the hall with his coat on, backwards and forwards, muttering to himself. Alice was beside herself with worry and kept asking him what was wrong, but thankfully he had understood my little story and kept his stupid drooling mouth shut. Then he started to cry, and Alice took him back to the home. Later, when I pointed out the wisdom of my decision not to accommodate an overgrown baby who was clearly disturbed, she walked out of the house and didn't come back for three days. Her first act of rebellion. I knew she would be back though. I never doubted it. She loved me too much. I never had to see the buffoon again, though Alice persisted in visiting him.

Once Eugene was out of the way, I settled down into a routine, although in 1993 this was disturbed by Moya, who had moved in next door. She and her dull husband befriended us straight away. I flatter myself that Moya was impressed by my celebrity. She was apparently something of a celebrity herself, having appeared in a television soap opera, but I had no idea who she was.

From very early on she flirted openly. There I would be at my desk in my study on a winter afternoon, painstakingly parsing every sentence, honing it to perfection. I would look up momentarily and Moya would be out in her garden, putting washing on the line, wearing nothing but a pink diaphanous gown and a pair of high heels. She must have been frozen. She would catch me looking, and scurry inside, feigning embarrassment, but Moya is a truly awful actress and it was painfully obvious that she intended to seduce me. I'm not terribly surprised. Her husband was such a nondescript nonentity that I cannot think of a single interesting thing he ever said or did. Occasionally I would see him in the garden, gardening.

In the summer months, Moya made an almighty display of herself, sunbathing nude on an extended sunlounger positioned perfectly to face my rear window. The view was rather nice, I admit it.

When we began our affair, she would write messages on large pieces of paper for me, and hold them up to her side window for me to see in a kind of semaphoric billet-doux. I was rather touched at the time. It seemed very sweet. We even managed to continue our arrangement while working abroad, most notably in New York, when she was to be in the Broadway version of *Solarand*. That ended in a huge bloody mess when Moya was fired and then almost caught me in the arms of the cute little actress who replaced her. You would swear that Moya was the wronged wife the way she went on about it, but I managed to talk her down and, after a while, we resumed our liaison.

Towards the end, the whole affair became stale and I redecorated the study again, reappointing the furniture so that my desk faced away from the windows. She was not happy about that. But I had my wife to consider, and I did not want Alice to be unnecessarily hurt.

At the very start I used a typewriter, but Alice often remarked on how little 'clacking' she could hear, so when word processors came on stream I used those, and now I have a turbo-charged state-of-the-art computer that allows me to work silently and stealthily. Of course, there is now a world of available distraction on the Internet and one could spend days on end looking at curiosities such as Victorian pornography or titanium drill bits, if one was so inclined. There is social networking too, Facebook and Twitter, which must be a curse to other writers, but suited me perfectly when I had time to waste.

However, when I was creating the *Prince of Solarand* series, the Internet the way we know it now had not been introduced, and there were far fewer distractions with which to fill my day. I would disappear into the study at 9.30 a.m., after breakfast, locking the door behind me. Peace and quiet and solitude. I would take up my *Irish Times* and begin with the Simplex crossword, moving on to the Crosaire. Then I would read the news, devouring every inch of the *Irish Times*, the *Guardian* and the *Telegraph*. I kept myself politically informed of the machinations of both the left and right wing, which gave me a rounded picture of what was going on, useful for punditry. (I am afraid that, as informed as I was, I did not see the economic crash coming. I lost at least a hundred thousand euro in poor investments – stupid bloody accountant – and I'm sure the Bulgarian properties are worth nothing, but I risked very little comparatively speaking.)

I would emerge at 11 a.m. for tea and biscuits and listen to the current affairs show on the radio for about half an hour. Then I returned to the study and attended to correspondence. Usually requests for media interviews and public readings; invites to literary festivals; letters from Ph.D. students using my opus as a basis for their theses:

Dear Mr Dax,

*I have found a great deal of allegorical evidence in your work which
would suggest that your children's stories are loosely based on the
Nazi persecution of the Jews prior to and during the Second
World War and wondered if I might trouble you for an
interview . . .*

I, and my complete works, have been the subject of no
less than eighteen academic theses, and several publications
have sought to deconstruct the stories. I have been deliberately unhelpful to these students, but they have persisted in
finding all sorts of hidden codes and meanings in my work.

Alice often suggested that I should engage a secretary.
'You have no time to deal with all that!' she said.

After lunch, I would read for an hour or two, the clas-
sics mostly, although latterly I had taken an interest in the
Old Testament of the Bible. I now have an extensive
library. I once overheard Alice say to Moya, 'I don't know
where he gets the time to read all of those books!' Where
did I find the time, indeed?

At one stage, out of boredom, I had some gym equip-
ment installed there to keep myself in shape. 'You're so
right,' Alice said, 'you need to have some distraction during the day!'

At 4 p.m., I would begin the actual work: one word at a
time, using several different dictionaries and thesauri, lay-
ing out the sentences again and again, reworking each
section several times until I came up with just the right
construction. I allowed myself just one hour a day at this
work. I had to make it last.

'You must be shattered!' Alice would say when I emerged from my laboratory, and I would agree and smile indulgently at her. Alice worked damn hard at her illustrations, and so I would sometimes cook for her and she would be grateful.

I do not mean to sneer at Alice. She made everything possible. Alice was always loyal. It is a wonderful quality in a wife.

13. Moya

I was shocked to my core when I heard what Oliver did to Alice. Everyone is talking about it. I mean, he was never the violent type as far as I knew, and if anyone should know, it's me. If it had happened before, Alice would undoubtedly have told me. I am so glad that I'm not around for the trial. Not all publicity is good publicity. Oliver certainly never raised a hand to me. I have seen him irritable all right, the man could be cranky for sure, and occasionally, towards the end of our relationship, he was downright rude to me, but in the early days he was very different.

I always thought Oliver could have done better than Alice. She just wasn't his type. That probably sounds ridiculous when you think how long they've been married, but anyone who met the pair of them together would have said the same thing. Well, they mightn't have said it, but they'd definitely have been thinking it. Anyway, he and Alice were not seen together out and about at openings and social functions that often, so I guess Oliver agreed with me. He said it was because she was shy. If I were her, I wouldn't have let him out of my sight.

I first met the Ryans when we moved into the house next door to them; it must be nearly twenty years ago now. Kate and Gerry were only toddlers at the time. It's strange to think that their house was Alice's family home, because it always seemed to me to be very much Oliver's territory.

I took the opportunity to introduce myself at their earliest convenience. At the time, I only knew Oliver as Vincent Dax. Con was reluctant to come with me; he's so backward about coming forward sometimes. But I insisted. Oliver himself opened the door to us. I nearly swooned. He really is such a handsome man. Dark and smouldering. Oliver really looked after himself over the years. We have so much in common.

I am sure there was an instant attraction between Oliver and me. Con was completely unaware of it at the time, as he is unaware of most things, I am sorry to say. I used to think that if only life were fair, Con would have ended up with Alice, and Oliver with me, and we all could have lived happily ever after. God knows I did my best to shove Con and Alice together over the years, but, alas, Con doesn't have the imagination to recognize an opportunity when he sees one. He'd probably bore her to death, but she was always so obliging that I'm sure she wouldn't have minded. It would have made it so easy for us. For Oliver and me.

Alice, despite being an artist, didn't look arty at all. She was frumpy, actually, and a bit on the heavy side. She wore mumsy clothes and had a collection of the most hideous cardigans I've ever seen, but she adored Oliver. You could see that a mile off. You could hardly blame her.

Con and I shared nothing but Sunday lunch. Con likes to eat. In his defence, I can tell you that he was always complimentary about my cooking. By the end of my first year of marriage to Con, I knew it was a mistake. I should have left him, but by then I was pregnant with Kate, and Gerry was born two years later. Con is a great dad, I'll give him that. He has always been patient with the children, and I really don't think I could have raised them on my own. He is dull, which is fine, if you like that sort of thing. Some women would be delighted to be married to him. He is a dentist. He earns a lot of money. He spends his working life looking into small, enclosed spaces filled with rot and decay. It genuinely interests him. That and gardening. When other dentists began to branch out a few years ago into cosmetic dentistry and Botox injections and derma fillers, could I persuade Con to get involved? No, I bloody couldn't. Like I said, no imagination. He could have saved me a fortune.

I really shouldn't be mean about him. I hate to be uncharitable. To me, he was like an unwanted pet. You don't want him around and yet you don't really want to hurt him or for him to come to any harm. He loves me, I suppose, and that is the cross I have to bear.

Oliver was just different in every way, but he was off-limits. That is what made it all so exciting. I knew he admired me. I had caught him watching me from the window of his study often enough. I knew it would not take much to seduce him. Sometimes, you just know.

It was sometime in the mid 1990s and I was starring as the Queen in the stage musical adaptation of Oliver's first book, *The Prince of Solarand*. Oliver sometimes appeared at rehearsals to see how things were going, or to consult on suggested changes to the text. Another writer, Graham, had been hired to write the libretto. Oliver was way too busy. Graham was delighted with how easy-going Oliver was about the script. Normally writers are unbelievably precious about changes or edits, but Oliver was fine about everything; even when quite substantial changes were made to some characters or plot points, Oliver was more than happy to go along with them.

After our first Saturday morning rehearsal, Oliver took a few of us to lunch in L'Étoile Bleue, a regular haunt of the acting community run by Michael and Dermot, who were Ireland's most famous gay couple. Oliver was generous. I had an easy familiarity with him by then, as we were neighbours, so it wasn't difficult for me to be able to monopolize him at the lunch. After the meal, it was only natural that Oliver would offer me a lift home. A little wine at lunchtime had loosened my self-control, and as we approached the Avenue, I found myself telling Oliver how attractive he was. I knew I was taking a risk. I was supposed to be a friend of Alice's, and he hadn't actually given me any reason to think he felt anything for me. So I was rather pleased to say the least when he put his hand on my thigh.

'Would you like to go for a spin?'

I can't claim that I didn't know what he meant. We continued to have the occasional 'spin' on a regular basis over the next two decades. In the early days, it was wildly exciting. It was my first affair – well, the first that actually meant something. I fell badly for Oliver and fantasized endlessly about how our life would be if we could be together.

In 1996, the announcement was made that *The Prince of Solarand* was going to transfer to Broadway after successful runs in Dublin and London, and that Oliver was to be with us for the first few weeks. I really thought that this was my big opportunity. The initial run was to be six months with an option to extend if we proved successful. I was bound to get movie offers, and Oliver and I would leave our spouses and eventually move to LA and become Hollywood A-listers. Like Arthur Miller and Marilyn Monroe (if they'd lived happily ever after).

Oliver was being put up in the New York Plaza by his American publishers, who were schmoozing him and his agent about film rights while I and some of the other cast members were accommodated in rather grotty apartments in the East Village. Con wanted to come, of course. We had never been to New York. I told him there would be no point and that I would simply be way too busy to spend any time with him, rehearsing for the first week or two, and then in previews for another few weeks, and then eight shows a week after press night. I knew that Alice wasn't coming. She never accompanied Oliver on his publicity tours. Quite the home bird.

Despite getting rave reviews in Dublin and London, the Broadway producers/investors wanted some changes to the show. Big changes. Only five of us from the original Irish production were to reprise our roles. The chorus was to be all American. We would be working with a new American director, Tug Blomenfeld. Aisling, our Irish director, was furious but had little or no say in the matter and was forced to take a back seat while Tug set about reblocking scenes and demanding totally unnecessary changes to somehow justify his enormous fee. Right from the start, Tug and I did not hit it off, particularly because the first time I met him, I mistook him for a wardrobe assistant at my costume fitting and handed him my tights to deposit in the laundry hamper. He was affronted and refused to laugh it off like a normal person. Our relationship went from bad to worse. He attempted to cut a lot of my lines and

had me hidden upstage half the time behind pieces of furniture or large props so that the audience wouldn't see me.
He tried to get me to sing the finale song in a different key,
which did not suit my voice. In front of the entire cast, he
told me to stop 'hamming it up'. The shit.

I suppose it was whispered within the company that I
might be seeing Oliver, not that anybody ever said it to my
face, but there were a few heavy hints and awkward silences
when we would arrive together at the theatre or the
rehearsal room. I complained bitterly to Oliver about the
changes that Tug was making, but Oliver insisted that he
had no influence and there was nothing he could do.

The rehearsal period was intense, but we did manage to
snatch a few hours off together now and then. They were
wonderful afternoons and we had rather a good time doing
the usual touristy things: the Empire State, the Rockefeller
Plaza, the Guggenheim, the Met, the Frick, a horse and
carriage around Central Park. One night we had dinner in
Sardi's. Oliver just automatically knew how to bribe the
maître d' to get us a good table. I was very impressed.
Then I spotted Al Pacino at the table behind us. I wanted
to go and introduce myself, but Oliver insisted we leave
him alone. He did, however, swap places with me so that I
was facing Al. I tried to catch his eye, but to no avail. I
went to the Ladies a few times so I could walk past him,
but I'll have to assume that he didn't know who I was, despite the fact that my face was plastered on a life-size poster
just two blocks away. Oliver found all this very amusing. At
the end of the meal, as we were exiting the restaurant, the
maître d' passed me a note. When I opened it up, it said,
'Good to see you, kid. Best of luck with the show – Al'! I

just about died and was all prepared to run back in to thank Mr Pacino, but Oliver point-blank refused and much later admitted that he'd paid the maître d' to write the note. I felt a bit silly and was initially disappointed, but I have to admit that it was a kind thing to do. That's the sort of man I thought Oliver was. Charming and thoughtful.

Oliver was exceptionally good company. He is very well read and knows about everything, so that an otherwise dull trip to an art gallery was turned into an endlessly interesting potted history of the artists' lives or a social commentary upon the time in which the work was created. He had a quirky sense of humour too, and he just looked like a celebrity. Doormen and waiters always deferred to him. He has an air of authority unusual in Irish men. Confidence.

New York is so buzzy, so full of life at its best and worst and weirdest. It could have been a bit more romantic, I suppose, if Oliver had held my hand or something, but he was never the touchy-feely type and displays of affection were kept behind the bedroom door. I tried to get to really know him in depth on our days out, asking about his childhood or his family, but he would change the subject or get distracted and I got the distinct impression that he didn't like talking of his past. To my annoyance, he talked rather a lot about Alice – how skilful her illustrations were, how much of an effort she was making to improve her culinary skills, or how she respected him and always consulted him before making a large purchase. It was infuriating, actually, how easily he could sing her praises and kiss me hungrily all in the same minute. I'd never met somebody before who could compartmentalize his life in such an unfeeling manner. And yet it was so bloody attractive. I bit my tongue and agreed about what a little treasure Alice was as I draped my leg around his neck.

At work, as we approached our first public performances, things became more difficult. After the first preview, all but one of my scenes in the first act were cut, as was my big solo number after the interval. Marcus, who was playing Grimace, got an entirely new song, and the first act was now going to end with the special effects' stunt flying-chair sequence instead of my big entrance with the chorus behind me. I was incandescent. The Irish producers avoided me and refused to make themselves available for meetings. The Americans were putting up the money and could do what they liked. After the tenth call back home, even my agent began to make excuses not to talk to me. Oliver had flown out to LA for another series of meetings and wasn't due back until opening night. The other actors, seeing I was out of favour with Tug, kept their distance from me, for fear that my unpopularity was contagious, and I realized that I was very much alone. After a few gins one evening, I even rang Con and cried down the phone at the unfairness of it all.

On the day of the opening night, I was called to the theatre at 8 a.m., a ridiculous time to call an actor. I grew suspicious when I realized that everyone else's call time was 11. I badgered the stage manager and demanded to know what was going on. She claimed not to know.

When I arrived at the theatre, I was ushered into a meeting room that contained nearly all of the senior producers of the show, amid whom sat Tug. Smug Tug.

'We've decided to recast the role of the Queen,' said Tug.

'I beg your pardon?'

Aisling was sitting beside him, her head down, fiddling with her notes and looking uncomfortable, as well she might.

'We'd like to thank you for your work and dedication, but I know I speak for us all when I say that we need a queen with a little more . . .' Tug was lost for words.

'Energy!' said one of the Americans helpfully.

Tug was encouraged. 'Yes,' he said, 'we feel that this role is just too much for someone of your . . .' He looked me straight in the eye and relished the word. 'Age.'

I don't fully recall everything I said to the assembled bunch of arseholes, but I did leave the room screaming, 'Fucking amateurs, the lot of you!'

Aisling hustled me into a cab and said she'd deal with it. My agent thankfully managed to stop the story going public, but only on condition that I did not sue Tug or any of the producers. They put out the usual story about exhaustion coupled with a recurring throat infection; I had 'graciously stepped down from the role and wished Shelley Radner (twenty-three), former member of the chorus, every success with her Broadway debut'.

Aisling and the Irish producers tried to apologize, ducking the blame. As with everything showbiz, it was all about the 'biz' and not about the 'show'. Tug wanted me out, and he had more control over the wallet than any of my own team. I was sure he was sleeping with Shelley.

I went back to my apartment and drank what was left of everybody's duty-free. I tried calling Oliver at the Plaza, but he wasn't there. I even tried calling Con in Dublin again, but there was no answer. I passed out but woke up at 10 p.m. with a splitting headache and a need for revenge.

I headed out again towards the theatre. The show had just come down and the audience were streaming out past the hastily reworked posters in which my head had been replaced by Shelley's (twenty-three). They were smiling and humming the finale song. The show was going to be a hit. The musicians were standing smoking outside the stage door, and I faltered a moment, wondering if this time I was the punchline of their never-ending innuendo. At that moment the stage door opened and Shelley emerged, followed by Oliver, whose arm was casually squeezing her shoulder in an obvious gesture of familiar intimacy as she buried her face in his neck. I was about to physically attack both of them when I felt a tap on my shoulder and turned to find a jet-lagged and bewildered-looking Con clutching a large bunch of red roses.

'Surprise!' he said.

I vomited.

Con and I left New York together the next day. He was very kind about everything in his annoying way, assuring me that Broadway was all about money and not about art.

'Sure, what do we want New York for? Haven't we got Gerry and Kate and each other and the garden?'

I hid away for a few days, aghast at the double betrayal. My profession and my lover. Yes, yes, I was cheating on Con, Oliver was cheating on Alice, but I thought we were cheating *exclusively*, and that we meant something to each other. Alice called in to the house a few times, bearing casseroles, as if someone had died. It was somewhat appropriate. I certainly thought my career had expired and I was going to murder Oliver the next time I saw him.

It practically kills me that Shelley got to play the Queen when they made the big screen version, the only one of the Broadway cast to reprise their role on film. She was nominated for a fucking Oscar for it, but Meryl got it again that year, God bless her.

Oliver arrived home just three weeks after me. Alice went happily to collect him from the airport and I watched as he got out of the car and went up the steps to his front door, seemingly without a care in the world. I waited three days for him to ring or call to the house. There was absolutely no way I was going to beg for his attention again.

On the fourth day, I could bear it no longer. Con was at work and I saw Alice driving out the front gate, as usual almost taking the gatepost with her. I knew he was alone in the house.

I wanted to look my best for this showdown and prepared myself carefully, buffing, tweezing, and dressing in my most alluring garb.

Oliver answered the door and whistled admiringly as he took in the view.

'Darling, how have you been? I've been waiting for the opportunity to call.'

'Shelley?' I spat, unable to control my anger. 'You were fucking Shelley?'

Oliver flinched. He hated bad language, but he also looked puzzled.

'Shelley . . .' he said, as if trying to recall who she was. 'What are you talking about?'

'Don't lie to me, Oliver! I saw you with her coming out the stage door.'

'Oh, *that*? Don't you see? I was just trying to make sure Con wouldn't suspect you and me!'

I was confused for a moment.

'Con told me he was coming to New York to surprise you. I tried to put him off but he insisted, and I was worried he suspected something was going on between us, so I thought it would be better if he thought that I was seeing someone else. It was all such a mess. I didn't get a chance to tell him you'd been fired because he was in the middle of the Atlantic at the time. I knew he was going to be waiting for you at the stage door after the show, so I made sure to come out with some dolly bird on my arm and Shelley was closest.'

I was not entirely sure whether to believe him or not – after all, he lied with such ease to Alice – but he took my hand and raised it to his lips and kissed the tips of my fingers. I realized that it didn't entirely matter whether it was true or not. I was not going to give him up. A wave of tension washed out of my head.

'Oh, Oliver,' I said. He kissed me then and led me upstairs, and I thought that maybe everything was going to be all right.

Our affair picked up where it had left off. In fact, it improved to the extent that I was emboldened after a few months to suggest that we might one day leave our respective spouses and set up home together.

'Don't be an idiot,' he said.

He made it clear that he would never leave Alice. He said that it wouldn't be fair to her. In the beginning I tried to make him see that he would be happier with me, that I would be good for him, that I would be a more suitable partner for somebody of his stature, but these pleas were met by silences that could last months and eventually I learned that if I wanted any part of him, I would have to do things his way.

My career picked up too, after a while. I was selected to be a team leader on a TV game show and I picked up a lot of voice-over work for commercials and radio dramas.

I know I said earlier that I was supposed to be a friend of Alice's. The truth is that I couldn't stand her. Not because of anything she did to me, but because she was in my way. I just wished she would disappear.

And now, in a sense, she has. I'm not proud of the way I felt towards her.

I don't think I have betrayed Alice. I would have in the past if Oliver had agreed to leave her. I would have betrayed her and not given it a thought.

She was useful though. I don't mind admitting that she was extremely helpful with my two children. When I was working long days in studio or in theatre rehearsals and Con was stuck in the clinic, Alice would often come over to be there when they got home from school. She said that Oliver needed absolute concentration to write his wonderful books; there was no question of the kids going over there, children were too much of a distraction. Alice was like an unofficial nanny for Gerry and Kate, actually. Sometimes when I got home she'd have a three-course meal prepared. It seems she got very interested in food after she was first married. Oliver told me that she grew up with a retarded brother who could only eat rice pudding and potatoes, and apparently she hardly knew what food was supposed to taste like until Oliver packed her off to a cookery school the week after they married. I confess that this stimulated my own interest in cooking. I can hardly believe that I felt forced to compete with bloody Alice. On the rare occasions when Con was away and I could entertain Oliver at home, I liked to be able to feed him in the manner to which he was accustomed.

You would think that Alice and I might have had more in common. After all, we were both in love with the same man. We were thrown together in all sorts of ways. I initiated the 'friendship', actually; it seemed the easiest way to get close to Oliver. But, my God, she drove me mad with her slow, dreamy ways and her nonsensical conversation. I dreaded the occasional afternoons that I would have to spend in her company. I always tried to come up with an activity that would keep her busy, would negate the need for much conversation: cinema, shopping, theatre.

Of course, I feel bad about it all now. The last time I saw Alice was in Bordeaux airport last November, just a few days before Oliver lost it with her. She was really upset. At the time, I thought she was upset about Javier and me. No doubt we'll find out the whole truth during the trial.

Maybe I should have been nicer to Alice and maybe I shouldn't have slept with her husband for nearly twenty years, but a small part of me wishes that the fight was about me. I wonder if he ever truly cared about me. Or her.

14. Oliver

When I was young, very young, before that summer in France, I tried hard to be a good person. I spent most of my life trying to impress a man who more or less refused to acknowledge my existence. My birth certificate names my mother as 'Mary Murphy (maiden surname)', probably one of the most ubiquitous names for a Dublin female at the time. It states that my parents were unmarried. Over the years, private research has yielded absolutely nothing about her, and I could only speculate that this was not her real name. My father is listed as 'Francis Ryan'. Under 'Rank or Profession of Father', it says 'priest'. I realize that it must have been a scandal in 1953, or would have been, if it hadn't been hushed up in some way.

My place of birth on the certificate is 'Dublin', although I do not appear in any register of births for maternity hospitals or nursing homes in the city, and because of that I can't be sure that my date of birth is accurate. Two Mary Murphys gave birth on that date in the city. I have gone to great lengths to find them and their offspring and rule out any possible relationship to me.

I wonder how there could be no trace of her. I know it was a different time, but how could this document have been approved? The church's stranglehold on the state was certainly strong in those days, but this was deliberate obfuscation. I once had the courage to ask my father about my mother and the circumstances of my birth. 'She was a whore,' he wrote, in reply to my letter, as if that was all the explanation that was needed. It wasn't too long before I got to hear a most bizarre version of the circumstances of my birth, but my father had to die before that tale could be spun.

One day, in March 2001, I was casually reading Saturday's *Irish Times* and came across my father's death notice in the paper.

'. . . *deeply regretted by his loving wife, Judith, and son, Philip . . .*'

I was not sure how to feel about this news. I was not sad, certainly; maybe a little relieved. I had long ago accepted that he did not want me in his life, but the slimmest hope was always there that he might one day find it in his heart to forgive me for whatever he thought I had done, that he might take pride in my success and claim me as his own. Now that the hope was gone, perhaps I could relax.

The wording of the notice hurt me unexpectedly though. I was also his son, but did not merit a mention.

The Funeral Mass was the following Monday morning. My curiosity got the better of me. I told Alice that I had a meeting in town and went to Haddington Road church. I lurked at the back, avoiding the glances of parishioners who might recognize me. Now was not the time for autograph hunters. There was a substantial turnout, a flurry of priests, a bench of bishops and a cardinal. Judith was elegant and dignified, but grey, and Philip was ageing badly, unlike his mother, but wore a priest's collar, to my surprise. Ironically, I remember thinking that the family line would die with him.

When the time came, I shuffled forward with the herd to convey my condolences to the bereaved. Judith took my proffered hand wetly.

'Oliver!' she said, reddening and turning to Philip. 'Don't you remember Oliver . . . from school?'

Philip looked up, and I saw that his eyes were filled with tears and misery, and I wondered how he could feel that way. I could tell that he was confused by my attendance.

'Of course, yes, thank you for coming. I heard you are an author now?'

'A writer, yes,' I said. 'Children's books.'

'Yes.'

The line of mourners was building behind me and I knew that I must move on.

'I'm sorry for your loss,' I managed to say.

Father Daniel from St Finian's was smoking a pipe outside the church. He greeted me warmly and thanked me for the annual donation I made to the school.

'I'd say that was hard for you . . .' he said.

'Judith and Philip . . . do they even know that I am his son?' I tried to keep the tremor from my voice.

'I think Judith knows.' He shook his head. 'The death notice . . . that was your father's wish. I'm sorry. He didn't want any reference to you.'

Father Daniel offered his condolences to me, and it was kind of him, but I did not need them.

'I wasn't sure if you'd be here. I was going to ring you. Come and see me next week. There's something I need to explain to you. About your father.'

15. Philip

I wish I had never discovered that Oliver was my brother. Half-brother. I can't conceive of how he could attack a woman like that, let alone his own wife. I am appalled. I have looked into my heart and have prayed about it. I know I should try to make contact with him again, but I am just not ready. Not yet. Fortunately, so far, nobody knows of our relationship and I think it best that it stays that way. Perhaps if we had grown up together, his life could have turned out very differently.

My home was fairly traditional. Financially, we were comfortably off, but lived sensibly without being austere. The only visible concession to our status was the family car, always a Mercedes. We lived in an average-sized house in a respectable suburb, chosen, I think, for its convenience to my school. I was raised as an only child, doted on by both parents. I didn't miss siblings since I didn't know what it was like to have them. When I was old enough to observe other families, I felt glad that I had my parents to myself and didn't have to share their attention. My mum and dad were happily married and seldom rowed, though they lived quite separate lives. Both of my parents were religious, my father maybe more so than my mother. Mum was soft, letting me get away with all sorts of things, and protected me from Dad when she knew he might disapprove of my actions. Dad was a more complex character. He could be strict, but I think he was fair. Mum was more gregarious than Dad and enjoyed going out to concerts and the theatre, and other social activities. Dad more often stayed at home with a book or a wildlife programme on TV. He didn't like socializing much. I can remember us hosting only two parties in my childhood, and my father's awkwardness on each occasion was palpable. He seldom drank, and avoided the company of drunk people. I admired him greatly, and though I love my mother dearly, I am more inclined to his way of living.

I was a serious boy, quiet and contemplative and generally obedient. My parents liked to boast that I gave them 'no trouble'. I was better than the average student, not terribly sporty, but a 'trier'. I made friends easily and was often chosen as class captain. Mum stayed at home and Dad went to work every day as a senior accountant in the Archbishop's Palace. My father had been a priest before he met my mum. It wasn't that unusual to have a father who was an ex-priest. A lot of men of that vintage joined the church as a matter of pride to their families before realizing that they didn't truly belong. My mum was the niece of the bishop under whom he served. I always assumed that my dad's attraction to my mum was what made him leave the church, but we didn't really speak about such things at home. He was always so priestly in his ways that I often wondered if he regretted leaving the priesthood. I asked him about it once when I was older, but instantly regretted it when he sighed and changed the subject. Mostly, he was an affectionate dad, but particularly when I was good. My misdemeanours were met by lectures, which were followed by long silences. Early on I learned that if I wanted forgiveness, I must ask for it.

I was a bit scared of Oliver Ryan at school. He was years ahead of me in the senior school when I was very small and we hardly had any interaction, but I remember him particularly well because of his odd behaviour. The senior and junior school shared a hall and some playing fields, so I came across him from time to time and I didn't like the way he stared at me. I always felt he was about to speak to me, but no, he never spoke, just stared. It was creepy to a seven- or eight-year-old. He was tall and strong-looking, but stood out as scruffy, I suppose. His uniform didn't ever fit properly: trousers too short or elbows visible through threadbare sweaters. I tried not to pay much attention to him, and contrived to stay out of his way. We shared a surname but there were a few others with the same name so I didn't think anything of it. He was a full-time boarder while I was a day-boy.

One Friday lunchtime, I was sent on an errand to the senior school by a teacher to deliver a message to the science master in the lab on the top-floor corridor. As I passed a window, I realized there was rather a good view of my house and I stopped momentarily to have a look before I continued on my way; but when I returned on the same route a little while later, I passed Oliver, who was standing at the same window, a pair of binoculars raised to his eyes. His jaw was set in concentration and he did not notice as I scurried past him, but a backward glance confirmed what I instinctively suspected. The binoculars were trained on my home. He was spying on *my house*.

When I went home after school that day, I tried to

forget about it, but I was spooked and disturbed. After we had said grace at the dinner table, as Mum was dishing out the meal, I raised the subject.

'There's a boy in the senior school who was spying on our house today.'

'I think you've been reading too many comics,' Dad said, barely raising his head from the usual file of ecclesiastical notes.

'No, really,' I said. 'He was watching our house through binoculars.'

Mum was interested at least.

'A senior boy? He was probably just birdwatching or plane spotting.'

'No,' I insisted, 'he was definitely looking at this house.'

My father paused and looked up from his notes.

'Do you know this boy's name?'

'Oliver. Oliver Ryan.'

There was a definite frisson at the table. What had I said? Mum looked at Dad, and then down at her lap.

'What? Do you know him?'

My father bit his bottom lip, and sat back from the table. 'What is it?' I asked. 'Are we related?'

Without a word, my mother got up from the table and started clearing away the soup bowls, even though we had only just started eating. She noisily clattered spoons and condiments together as she disappeared into the kitchen.

'He is a distant cousin,' my father said. 'I want you to have nothing to do with him.'

A cousin! I had only two cousins on my mother's side and none on my father's.

'But why? Is there something wrong with him? What did he do? Is he bad?'

My father suddenly grew angry. I had never seen him so worked up before.

'Do not question me about this. The boy is from bad stock. You are too young to understand, but his mother was bad news, as, I'm sure, is he. We will not discuss him again. Just keep away from him.'

Startled by his sudden anger, I burst into tears. At once, my father regretted his loss of temper. He ruffled my hair with his large hand and patted my face. He said then, in a gentler tone, 'Let's have no more about it.'

My tears subsided, and my mother re-entered the room. The subject was swiftly changed to that of the neighbour's new dog, and I was cheered when Dad suggested that I might have a dog on my next birthday.

That night, however, I could hear a muffled row between my parents downstairs. A door was slammed. The next morning, everything was as normal.

My curiosity was piqued, however. My mother stone-walled my queries, insisting that I should not ask any further. I asked around at school. Most people thought that Oliver's parents were dead. It was known that he didn't go home during holidays. Some suggested that he was a scholarship student from an orphanage, which might explain his deprived appearance. Sometimes, at home, I would wave out the window in the direction of the school, in case he was watching. He never gave any indication of having seen me, and even though he continued to stare, I felt more kindly towards him. There was something vaguely romantic about having an orphaned cousin. I didn't get far with my enquiries, and when Oliver left the school just a year or two later, I forgot all about him.

I think I always knew I was going to be a priest. Of course my home life was very Catholic and that was undoubtedly a big influence, but the sacraments meant something to me. I enjoyed the rituals and, unlike most children, for me Easter was a bigger event than Christmas, the idea of the ultimate sacrifice and resurrection far more appealing than toys or Santa Claus. My father was pleased that I took such an interest in church matters, and encouraged it. Mum was less happy about it. I think she would have liked me to settle down with a girl and produce a brood of grandchildren. She tried to dissuade me from my chosen course. It was the source of a rare argument between my parents.

I dated some girls and experimented sexually, but it felt somehow like a betrayal of my faith, a rude distraction from what I knew was going to be my path. The word 'vocation' is often used as something mystical; you hear of 'messages from God' or lightning bolts or a simple 'feeling', but my decision to join the seminary was based on something far more prosaic. The fact was that I didn't really want to do anything else. I wanted to work in a parish, to help and to serve a congregation, celebrate Mass, administer last rites. I had been volunteering in my church since I was a boy, and the priests there were men I looked up to and admired. Contrary to popular belief, I am neither scared of nor insecure around women. I enjoy their company enormously. I just have no need of a wife or children. Nor am I gay, as my mother speculated. I am happy to be celibate. Dad was absolutely delighted when I told him I wanted to join the seminary. Nothing, he said, could have made him prouder.

A few years later, when I was in the seminary, I found a photograph of Oliver Ryan in the newspaper. He was a publishing 'sensation'. I recalled that he was a Ryan cousin but he was now going by the name of Vincent Dax. I mentioned it to my father when he next visited and asked him to explain the relationship that he hadn't been able to explain to a small boy. Dad was still clearly uncomfortable with the subject. He told me that Oliver's mother had been a woman of 'ill repute'. I questioned the Ryan connection; it must have been Oliver's father who was related to us, surely? Dad looked away and said that Oliver's father had died young of tuberculosis. I knew that he was lying to me. I suspected that if Oliver's mother had been a prostitute, perhaps his father had died of syphilis or some other sexually transmitted disease, and that my father wanted to hide the details. Seeing his unease, I moved the conversation along and asserted that at least it was good to have a famous author in the family. Dad actually flinched and suggested that if I wanted a successful career in the church hierarchy, it would not do to associate myself with a family scandal. I could see his point.

Still, as Vincent Dax's notoriety grew, I followed the media coverage of his success. I even bought one of his books. It was very good indeed. So I was quietly proud of my cousin, but kept our relationship to myself.

On the day of my ordination, nobody was happier than my father. I was very glad to bring him such joy. We were always close, Dad and I. Like-minded in many ways,

I suppose. He spent more on my ordination celebrations than he would have on a wedding, and insisted on paying for handmade robes. My mother, red-eyed, put her objections aside and genuinely wished me well.

I still find it impossible to believe that my father lied for so long about something so fundamental. Even on his death-bed, he couldn't tell me the truth. It's nearly eleven years ago now since I discovered the facts, and even then . . . how can I know for sure? The only person who knew with certainty is gone.

My father was diagnosed with pancreatic cancer just six weeks before his death. His suffering was thankfully short-lived and he knew it was terminal. I was coincidentally the chaplain appointed to the hospice where he spent his last weeks. It meant that I was able to be with him, sit with him and pray with him. Chemotherapy might have given him more time, but he declined it, choosing quality over quantity of life. His pain was managed well with medication, and he received visitors with grace and dignity. At the very end, when it was clear that it would be just a matter of days or hours, my mother and I kept vigil with him, both of us straining to maintain a tone of optimism though we knew it was hopeless. He was still conscious when I administered the last rites, or the Anointing of the Sick, as the sacrament is known.

For me, it is the most meaningful of all the sacraments. It is about giving the patient the strength, peace and courage to endure pain and suffering, it is to find unity with the passion of Christ, it is spiritual preparation for the passing over to eternal life and it is the forgiveness of sins. My father accepted my words and bowed his sunken head in prayer, but my mother, on the other side of the bed, took his arm and stroked it.

'Francis? Is there anything you would like to tell Philip?'

I was confused, and a little annoyed with my mother for disturbing such a peaceful moment. My father grew agitated. He shifted in his bed and I moved some pillows underneath his shoulder in order to make him more comfortable. He closed his eyes and exhaled. I looked at my mother quizzically.

'Francis,' she said again gently, smoothing his furrowed brow, 'it is time to tell.'

My father turned his face into the pillow away from both of us, and I could tell from the shaking form under the bedclothes that he was crying. I was distressed at seeing my father in such misery and berated my mother. Whatever it was, now was certainly *not* the time. I called a nurse, who upped the morphine dose in his drip. He relaxed then and we were able to take his hands again until he slipped into unconsciousness. A few hours later, he passed over. It was almost dawn.

The day after my father's funeral, my mother told me that Oliver Ryan was my half-brother. She had desperately wanted my father to be the one to tell me, but right to the end he was deeply ashamed. Mum said he had got a woman pregnant while a priest back in the 1950s. She may have been a nurse, or even a nun. My mother doesn't think she was a prostitute like my father told me, back when he was maintaining that Oliver was a cousin. My father never revealed the mother's name. Mum says the woman abandoned her baby and disappeared, never to be seen again.

My father told my mother about it in the early days of their relationship. He insisted on starting their marriage with a clean slate and had Oliver shipped off to St Finian's to be raised by the priests. Mum thought Dad was wrong to do that.

My mother was not the reason why Dad left the priesthood. They met some years later. She says that he was resistant to their relationship in the beginning; she thinks that they eventually bonded over their shared faith and that it was only when her uncle, Dad's former bishop, gave his approval that Dad allowed himself to actually fall for her. He still kept extremely close links to the church and ultimately worked for them.

My mother insists she would have raised Oliver as her own son, if Dad had let her. Mum says that it was the only thing that caused heartache in their marriage. It was simply a part of my father's life that he refused to acknowledge or discuss. She says he passionately and irrationally hated the boy, and she never knew why.

I was stunned to hear this, of course. How could the father I knew have abandoned a child so cruelly when he had always treated me with such warmth and affection? How could he have denied me a brother? Regardless of what Oliver's mother was like, how could he have hated an innocent child? My mother couldn't give me answers and nor could the priests of my father's acquaintance who might have been contemporaries. They either had no knowledge of the tale or had heard something of the story back in the day, but none could add further information. Shockingly, Oliver knew that we shared a father. How jealous must he have been of me? The staring and the spying in my schooldays finally made sense. Oliver Ryan was only watching his family. If the betrayal I now felt was so great, how must Oliver have felt his entire life? Earlier the previous day, I had accepted condolences from my brother on our father's death. I knew that at some stage in the not too distant future, I would need to seek out this stranger. Perhaps it was not too late to welcome him to the family.

When I did seek him out some months later, our meeting did not go well.

16. Oliver

I was intrigued by Father Daniel's cryptic words at my father's funeral. I wondered if my father had left me a bequest or a message of some kind, and I was conflicted about whether I wanted to receive it. But Father Daniel had always been good to me and I wanted to see him.

Father Daniel was a great age at this point, but his mind was still sharp and the years had not dulled his compassion. I know my current circumstances would be a great disappointment to him if he were still alive, but perhaps, of all people, he might have understood my desperation.

I was led into the priest's parlour, familiar from the few occasions of my father's visits in school days. It had not changed at all. I could see at once that Father Daniel was agitated, and he began by telling me that he was not sure if he was doing the right thing.

'Your father was a . . . strange man,' he stated, and got no argument from me. 'I wanted to . . . I'm not sure if . . .' There was his hesitancy and uncertainty again.

It seemed there was no bequest. I was not upset about that. It was not as if I needed money at that stage. Father Daniel explained that my father's estate had been left entirely to Judith and Philip. I was not mentioned in the will. Judith had subsequently given Father Daniel a box containing some gold holy medals that she asked him to pass on to me. I examined them in their box. They were engraved with crucifixes.

Father Daniel tried to apologize on my father's behalf. I brushed off the apology and accepted a small glass of Jameson to lessen the priest's embarrassment.

'Did he ever mention to you . . . ? About your mother?' He looked nervous as he said it.

I sat up straight. 'My . . . mother?' Even the words felt alien on my lips.

He shifted position in his chair. 'I see, I thought not. It's not easy . . .' he began, 'we don't have to . . . if you don't want to.'

I asked for a minute and left the room, and had the strongest urge to smoke as my hands began independently to reach for my cuff buttons. I paced the corridor outside and was tempted just to walk away. Did I need this, did I really need to know? Of course I did. Every boy, regardless of age, needs a mother. If he can't have her, he must at least know something about her. It is the natural order of things. Whether I needed to know was not the issue. I wanted to know. I paused before I re-entered Father Daniel's room, wondering if I would be a different man when I emerged. I asked Father Daniel to tell me everything.

'I'm sorry,' he said, 'but I can only tell you what was said at the time. I have no proof of any of it, but I had friends out there at the time and they told me.'

'Out there?' I didn't know what he meant.

'Northern Rhodesia, now Zambia,' he said. 'There was an official report, but it was all hushed up. I tried to find it over the last month so that I would have something to give you, but it has disappeared. There are no records.'

These are the 'facts', as they were told to me:

My father was a young missionary priest who was sent out with three others to establish Catholic schools in rural villages along the Zambezi River in the early 1950s. In a particularly deprived and destitute village called Lakumu, where he was stationed for a year, he formed a friendship with a local native girl called Amadika.

Oh, no. My father was a paedophile priest? Oh, no. What has this to do with me?

Father Daniel was at pains to insist that Amadika was *not* a child. She was perhaps in her late teens or early twenties. They had a platonic relationship. She was apparently a very smart and diligent student, and it was known that my father favoured her with school prizes and allowed her to cook and clean for him.

He used her as his slave? Is that it? What has this to do with me?

The school was heavily oversubscribed, and a rule was introduced that only the younger children could attend. Amadika's mother begged my father to allow her to continue her studies, but my father refused. He could not break the rules for anybody.

Apparently, Amadika was sent by her mother to sexually seduce my father in order to bargain for her right to stay in school. Father Daniel says that the natives had nothing else with which to bribe their educators, and the girl's mother hoped that a good education might secure her future. It seems that my father was a particularly devout priest with ambitions, but that on this one occasion he yielded to natural urges and slept with the girl. He rejected her immediately afterwards, banned her from the school and ended their association.

Of course he slept with her. She offered herself. And then he was ashamed. What does this have to do with me?

Amadika's pregnancy caused a scandal when she claimed that Father Francis Ryan was the child's father. He strenuously denied it until the girl gave birth to a purely white baby – me.

No.

Impossible. No.

At this point in Father Daniel's narrative, I reeled first with disbelief, and later, shock. I had always assumed, because of what my father had said, that I was the result of an affair with a prostitute, and so had never wanted to explore the issue too deeply, especially after my birth certificate seemed to be a work of fiction, but this was just too fantastical to be credible, I thought. I was white. Father Daniel admitted that he too had found it difficult to come to terms with, but swore this was the story he was told by the other priests. He insisted that Amadika was not a prostitute but rather a person forced by poverty, desperation and circumstance to use the only thing she had at her disposal to make a better life for herself. Somehow, that rang a bell with me, but I simply could not accept it.

'You have no proof!' I whispered. 'You said there are no records!'

'There are none,' he admitted, 'but I really can't imagine why those who told me would lie about such a thing. I am the only person left alive who can tell you.'

I paced the room, processing what I had just been told, but it made no sense.

'Maybe I was wrong to tell you, but I thought you should know what was said. It was kept very quiet.'

I did not believe it, and told him so in no uncertain terms. He apologized for causing any distress, and I could see that he was in anguish about having told me such a tale.

'You can just carry on as normal. It is only we who know.'

'What happened? To her?'

I tried to make sense of a tale that made no sense as Father Daniel continued his story. My story?

Amadika rejected her baby straight away. Nobody in the village had ever seen a white baby before. She was terrified of it and shunned by her friends and her neighbours in the village, who thought that the baby's pale sickliness had brought a curse upon the tribe. Apparently, she left the child at the door of my father's hut and left the village with her mother. Nobody knows where she went. Nobody knew her last name.

My father had a mental breakdown. According to the other priests, he had been particularly devout. Father Daniel suggested that my father must have found it exceptionally difficult to have broken his vows. He was insistent that he had never initiated sexual contact. His lofty ecclesiastical ambitions were ruined. He was forced out of the priesthood and returned to Ireland with his unwanted son. However, because of strong connections to the Archbishop's Palace, my father was hired as a financial adviser and was warned to keep me as removed from him as possible, so as not to raise questions or provoke a scandal. They assumed, as the baby grew, as *I* grew, that I would develop physical signs of my black roots, that my hair might curl or my nose might flare, but I confounded their expectations by maintaining my Caucasian appearance.

Most of those who knew of my existence were told I was an orphaned nephew, but my father subsequently met and married Judith within a few years and abandoned me to St Finian's.

If Father Daniel was right, if it was all true, I am a freak of nature. My eyes are dark brown and my pigmentation is a little more sallow than the average Irishman, but in every respect I am a white European. I chose not to believe it.

I told nobody, and when Father Daniel died a year later, I let the ridiculous story die with him. It made no difference to me now, and there was nothing I could do about the past. Who knows what went on in Africa? A little bit of private research revealed that my father had been in Northern Rhodesia at the time, and there was a village called Lakumu, but that was as far as I was prepared to go. It didn't matter.

The truth is that I deserved a better father. I found one in France, but, alas, he was not mine.

17. Véronique

I cannot remember how it was that we ended up taking Irish students that year. I knew little of Ireland, apart from their whiskey and some of their music. A cousin of a friend organized it, I think. I recall being sceptical as to how college-educated people could adapt to heavy manual labour, but they tried their best, I will say that for them, with varying degrees of success. We also agreed at that time to take on some South Africans who were keen to learn about the Bordeaux wines of our region, and we were to train them in viticulture and pay a small fee in exchange for their labour. Naturally, not all of my white workers were happy about working alongside the black boys, but my father, who was still a hero to our community, led by example. Without having to say anything, we were subtly reminded by him of the dire consequences of racial intolerance.

I was later ashamed that I did not make more enquiries into exactly who was going to come and how they would work. I had received a letter from a man in Stellenbosch who asked if he could send his son along with seven other labourers to learn about our grapes, so I was prepared for eight men to stay for two months. But then we got seven black boys, some very young, and one Afrikaner man named Joost, who was the only one who spoke French. It turned out that Joost was to inherit some land in the Western Cape and his father had decreed that he must plant it as a vineyard, but Joost did not want to do any actual work so he brought these seven poor men to France to learn how to do the work for him. He refused to let them stay in the lodgings arranged for everybody else and had them billeted in a barn in the village. He also did not pay them the fee they had earned and instead paid them with wine that we dispensed freely. I did not work this out right away. It was the other labourers who told me what was going on. They were uncomfortable with it, and when I saw for myself the cuts and bruises on some of the men, I was finally convinced that the stories of Joost's brutality were true and ordered him to leave. There was nothing I could do for those boys, who were little more than slaves. They had no education and no French, and we would not have work enough to keep them on beyond that summer. Papa and I sought them out the night before they left while Joost got drunk in the village. We gave them some money and food, and although they seemed terrified, one boy stepped forward to shake my hand and thank us. The other boys seemed stunned at his audacity.

By then, technically speaking, I oversaw everything to do with the estate, the chateau, the orchard, the olive grove and the winery, with terrific support from our friends and neighbours, but on a practical level I had appointed local managers Max and Constantine to run each division, friends and neighbours that we trusted. It amuses me now when I think about it, to realize that we were operating not unlike a kibbutz, or a commune in the English sense of the word, although I insisted that the family eat separately in the house each evening while the workers ate outdoors. I was adamant that the workers would not stay in the house overnight. Everything else was shared. I actively encouraged Papa to let me take control, and I think he passed over the reins with relief and slipped into a graceful retirement. He did, however, insist on taking Jean-Luc's education in hand. Jean-Luc was to start school in the autumn and his papi was determined that Jean-Luc would have a head start.

The role that I relished more than any was feeding the workers and I appointed myself as head of the kitchens, a task probably more menial than Papa would have liked for me, but it was the job that I wanted and the one in which I excelled. After the war, when we were left without servants, Tante Cécile had rolled up her sleeves and learned how to feed us good and nutritious food, and I learned my craft from her. She taught me all the basics of good rustic cuisine, and I prepared simple and wholesome meals for all our workers, relying as I did on my neighbours Max and Constantine to keep order in the fields and orchards.

Oliver and Laura were the first of the Irish workers who came to my attention. They were a very beautiful couple. Somebody ought to have painted them. He was astonishingly good-looking for an Irishman. Instead of the pale blotchy complexion of the others, his skin was smooth and his eyes full-lashed and shining. His girlfriend, Laura, was also dark-haired and clear-skinned, and very petite. I had many of the local girls working in the fields, but I wondered if this girl might be too delicate for such work.

Oliver spoke French well and translated for the others, and Papa quickly began to rely on him as the spokesperson for the group. Since the time of his incarceration, Papa had developed a tremor in his right hand and his handwriting had suffered. He asked Oliver for help with some paperwork. Oliver took an interest in Jean-Luc too, and before long the three boys had bonded completely, regardless of the barriers of age, language and experience. Papa requested that Oliver be assigned as his assistant, and I, never having refused Papa anything before, conceded as usual. The relationship between them was extremely close, extraordinarily quickly. It was as if Papa and Jean-Luc had found the one they had long been searching for. I thought then that I had been wrong to deny my son a father, that Papa would have enjoyed having a man around the house, so while I was not altogether happy about this sudden friendship, I tolerated it for Papa's sake. I did not know why Oliver had formed such a close bond with them. Presumably, he had a father of his own, but I admit to a little jealousy at having to share mine.

I was not the only person feeling jealous of this new bond. Oliver's girlfriend was furious about Oliver's promotion. He began to take his meals with the family in the house, at Papa's insistence and against my wishes, and Laura seemed particularly jealous of the fact that Oliver obviously preferred the company of an old man and a boy to hers. Jean-Luc adored him. Oliver played the rough-and-tumble games with him for which Papa had grown too old. When I eventually persuaded Jean-Luc to go to bed, Oliver was always included in his chatter of the day. I thought of Pierre and what a wonderful father he could have been, had he known of his son.

Laura had a brother called Michael, who turned up one morning out of the blue at the kitchen door to offer assistance with bread making. It was a serendipitous moment for all concerned, except for Anne-Marie, who was startled to see a big, pasty-faced Irishman in the kitchen, and got such a fright that she fell over and broke her arm. Anne-Marie was my Girl Friday in the kitchen, if one can justifiably describe a 77-year-old as a girl. She had been employed by the family since the first war, and I had asked for her help in the kitchens the previous summer, and we worked well together. She related to me the stories of my mother's legendary beauty and her generosity. I am constantly aware of how much I have to live up to with the legacy of my parents' goodness. On that day in 1973, Anne-Marie was finally persuaded for the first time to take a leave of absence while her arm healed. A 77-year-old bone, however, does not heal easily and I knew I must do without her for some months.

Michael, oblivious to the fact that he was the cause of the accident, was quickly enlisted, as lunch was to be served for thirty people at twelve o'clock, while poor Anne-Marie was taken off to the hospital. Luckily, Michael was clever, and as cookery is about demonstration and repetition, the language problem did not become an issue. However, I was astounded by how little he knew about food, how few ingredients he even recognized. Maybe it was true what they said about the Irish, that they ate only potatoes. Michael learned quickly and, what is more, he enjoyed it and was flamboyantly enthusiastic about every aspect of the process. I could not be certain that there was not some other agenda though, and one or two times I caught him looking at me as if I were a kind of unknown ingredient that he was not sure whether to peel, boil or plant.

One day, he flicked my hair out of my eyes rather clumsily, and it came to me suddenly that perhaps he had some kind of inclination to be a hairdresser, so I allowed him to play with my hair for a while. How stereotypical, I thought, a gay hairdresser. He was, quite obviously, gay.

His French was still quite halting, but when I precociously asked him about his sexuality, he had no problem understanding and crumbled instantly, weeping copiously. I realize now that this was his 'coming out' and that my words opened a floodgate of guilt, repression and confused identity. I ascertained that he was in lust with his friend Oliver, who was dating his sister Laura. *Catastrophe.* I assured him that I would tell nobody, and arranged for him to meet with Maurice, our neighbour, who was openly gay and spoke some English. I hoped that Maurice would be able to counsel Michael, so I was quite cross with him when it soon became apparent that he had taken Michael to a gay nightclub. I thought that might be rushing things, but what business was it of mine? They were adults, after all.

So now I knew Oliver and Michael well enough. Laura was the person who connected them, and soon she made her presence felt in my life too. She was a lovely girl, perhaps a little spoiled, but she hated the fact that Oliver and Michael were in the house and that she only saw them in the evenings, while all day long she was left with the others in the orchards, so when she collapsed one day and was stretchered up to the house, I was suspicious to put it mildly, thinking that this was a ploy to get into the house and attract some attention. But she was pale and sick. I was right to be suspicious, but not in the way that I thought.

I took her to the doctor in the village, and with her consent he told me that Laura was pregnant. I was initially annoyed. This was my first year taking migrant workers, and first there was the trouble with the Africans and now this. These employees were my responsibility, and clearly her thoughtless behaviour meant there had already been trouble. There have always been ways to avoid pregnancy, and I am not talking about abstention. I tried to be calm when I spoke to her. She was very tearful and afraid that I would ask her to leave the estate. I was not sure what to do. She begged me not to tell Oliver, fearful that this would spell the end of their relationship, although it was apparent to me that the relationship was practically over anyway. He had fallen in love with my family instead. I did not know what advice to offer Laura, so I offered none. She was from a strict Irish Catholic family. Despite the family chapel on our estate, Papa had raised me without a faith and without a need for the guilt in which other Catholics seemed to like to indulge. The options that might have been open to a faithless Frenchwoman would have been unthinkable to an Irish teenager. Laura was only nineteen years old, but she had to make her own decisions. Her brother Michael was concerned. She lied to him, telling him that she had some gastric flu. I allowed her to stay in the chateau for a few days, but then sent her back to the fields. I left it to her to make her choices. Just a few weeks later, I no longer cared. Not just about Laura, but about anything.

During the war, Papa ordered 100 gallons of paraffin for the lamps in the wine cellar so that the Jewish families who stayed there would not have to spend their waking hours in complete darkness. It was delivered at night by a friend in the Resistance who had good contacts in Paris. I know my father sold my mother's jewellery to pay for it, as gold was the only reliable currency at the time. When the house was raided in 1944, the Germans at first thought it was petrol and tried to fuel their trucks with it, but of all that they had destroyed in the house, the only things they left behind were the cans of paraffin, discarded in a lean-to shed adjacent to the library in the east wing of the chateau. Papa's bedroom was directly above the library. By 1973, the entire building had long since been wired for electricity. It had crossed my mind at some time to dispose of the oil, but my father, who had lived through two wars and was more conscious of rationing than me, insisted that we hang on to the oil, in case of another war or a simple breakdown of electricity, which he still did not entirely trust. It was a particularly dry and dusty summer. On the 9th of September 1973, it had not rained for eighty-four days, and temperatures were well above average for the time of year.

Jean-Luc alternated between sleeping in my room or his papi's. His own bedroom was rarely used. Both Papa and I had a small cot bed perpendicular to our own at the foot of our beds. It was very common at the time in French homes. If Papa was telling Jean-Luc a particularly good bedtime story, Jean-Luc could not be persuaded to return to my room. Sometimes the stories were a little bit scary and the walk from Papa's room in the eastern side of the house to mine in the west wing was too much of a challenge for him. Papa would stay until Jean-Luc nodded off, and then, as it seemed a little cruel to move him as he slept, we would let him spend the night there.

I do not know what started the fire. My father's pipe, a cigarette, a stray ember from the charcoal oven, we will never know. My memory of the night is quite unclear; I was woken by a noise like a strong wind rushing through the corridors, and then the sound of shouting. I thought I must be dreaming. Even when I got out of bed and looked out the window and saw the east wing in flames, it was so unreal and absolutely unexpected that I still did not comprehend how much of an emergency it was. I wandered through the smoke-filled hall in my nightdress before I fully understood the horror before me. When I was shocked out of sleep, I was disorientated and lost my sense of direction, but as I ran along the gallery towards what I thought was the east wing, the searing heat and smoke drove me back. I began to shout for my beloved father and son, but the only response I heard was a hiss and a crackle and the splintering and spitting of wood. I became hysterical and batted my way into the flames to get across the gallery to the eastern side of the house, but the floor beneath me was smouldering and I could smell my singed hair. When I realized I was at the top of the burning staircase, I knew I could go no further. I do not know how I burned my hands so badly. At the time, I did not even feel the pain. I do not recall how I got from the upper gallery to the courtyard, but I remember being restrained there by Michael as I kicked and bit him, trying to get away from him to rescue the only people in the world that I loved.

I did not know it then, but I later came to understand that Jean-Luc and his papi died of smoke inhalation, probably in their sleep. It is something of a comfort to me, as I spent months afterwards in the nightmare of imagination wondering if they had to watch each other burn to death, screaming for my help, after desperately trying to save each other.

The chaos of the night comes back to me in small pieces: the surprising sound of my own screams; the grasping arms of Michael and Constantine, who held me back from the flames; the smell of the fire and my own sweat; the women from the dorm crying; the men taking control and becoming important, busy men of action. Quite separately, I remember secretly pregnant Laura hysterical and clinging to Oliver, who seemed not to know she was there.

I was heavily sedated in the days that followed. I have no memory of the funerals, but they tell me I was there. I stayed in the house. The western side was structurally unaffected; there was some smoke damage, but it was minimal. The thick stone walls between the east wing and the hallway stopped the fire from reaching my side of the house. The kitchen, salon and my bedroom, among others, were intact. Hundreds of people came and went, bringing food, prayers, reassurances, blessings, and shared experiences of loss, but it was weeks before I began to see that my future was exactly what Papa had always feared for me.

Some of the labourers left shortly after the fire, apologetically bidding farewell: it was obvious that we could not pay them. The vineyard was abandoned, but the Irish students stayed for another month. Most of them had come to France for the experience rather than out of financial necessity. Michael was wonderful and readily took control of the kitchen. I had no interest in anything, and my hands would take time to heal. The others did their best to clear the wreckage of the east wing. They had to return to college then, as they had already missed the first weeks. Oliver was in shock and barely spoke to anyone. I admit that I resented his grief because I felt he had no right to it. He had known them for a matter of months, but they were my life, and I felt bitter anger every time I saw him sitting absently on the terrace steps with his head in his hands, as Laura tried to cajole him back to life like one of our vines.

When it came to their leaving, Laura asked me if she could stay. She confided that she had told Oliver about the pregnancy in a moment of desperation, hoping that it would shock him into some reaction, but that Oliver did not want to know and insisted that he would never be a father again. Again? What did he mean, 'again'? Laura explained that Oliver had a game with Jean-Luc where he and Jean-Luc pretended to be father and son, and that my father had taken part. I do not know if this was true, but maybe Oliver really felt that he had become Jean-Luc's father in a way, and Papa's son too. It was a foolish game, but finally I understood his pain and grief, and without ever speaking of it, I forgave Oliver.

I told Laura she could stay. I did not think that she would be with me for a whole year, or that she too would die soon afterwards. So much death.

18. Michael

Laura's moods were erratic in the months following her return from France. My parents were concerned. She returned to college that October of 1974, but dropped out again in November. And then, in the first week in December, she went missing.

I got a phone call in the restaurant on a Thursday morning from Mum to ask if I knew where she was. She'd gone to bed the previous night at about ten o'clock, but when Mum called her that morning, there was no answer. Her bed had not been slept in and nobody had heard her leave the house. We rang around friends and neighbours, but nobody had seen or heard from her. When she still hadn't returned on Friday morning, my mother was out of her mind with worry. Laura had been very calm when my mother last spoke to her on Wednesday morning, to the extent that Mum thought Laura had turned a corner. They'd talked about going shopping for a new pair of boots at the weekend. Mum had seen a pair that she liked, and thought they would suit Laura. Mum said they'd go into town together to a particular shop on Saturday. Laura said she was looking forward to going back to college and getting back to normal, admitted that the year in France had been a bit of an ordeal, and said that she should have come home with me. Mum reassured her that everyone understood, that once she got back into a routine, things would fall into place. We made Mum go over that conversation again and again, every mundane detail, but could find nothing sinister or disturbing about it. Except that the brand-new boots that Mum had admired were later found in a box in Laura's wardrobe, but not in Laura's size. In Mum's size, bought and paid for on Wednesday afternoon.

We started ringing round hospitals on Friday morning. How often does it happen, I wonder, that a person turns up in hospital amnesiac and unidentified? Not often enough, I imagine, for those of us looking for them. On Friday afternoon, the guards came to take statements. They wanted to put her photograph in the newspapers. The most beautiful photo I had was one I'd taken in France with my Agfa Instamatic. We had all been drunk. Laura was leaning her head on Oliver's shoulder. He was naked from the waist up. Her eyes were closed, and about one quarter of her face was hidden behind several wine glasses in the foreground. But she was smiling in the photo, as if she knew a secret that nobody else did. We agreed it was not suitable for publication, and Dad found a photo from Christmas the previous year, where she looked happy but serious. My parents were terrified of the glare of publicity that was about to descend. We are private people and to them, my sister's breakdown was dirty laundry.

The sun continued to rise and set, the grandfather clock ticked its metronome of misery in the hallway, cars drove past, and children could be heard laughing as they passed our gates, but there was a gaping hole in the centre of our lives, a huge question mark without an answer. The photo was due to be published in the newspapers and broadcast on TV on Monday, but on Sunday afternoon the guards called and asked Dad to come down to the station. We knew there had been a development, but Dad refused to let Mum accompany him. I waited with Mum while he was gone, and we speculated on what the breakthrough might be, both of us terrified of uttering what we already knew, as if by saying it, it made it real.

Dad returned a relatively short time later with Mum's brother, my Uncle Dan, and a young garda. I don't know why the garda came with him. Maybe it was policy. Maybe it was courtesy, to make sure Dad got home all right.

Laura's body had washed up on the Tragumna beach that morning in West Cork. A dog walker (why is it always a dog walker?) had seen someone the previous night from the cliff-side and had alerted the guards. Apparently she had walked into the sea fully clothed. We protested that it couldn't be her. Why would she go there? But really we knew that was exactly where she'd go. It was the beach we had played on as children when we visited my maternal grandmother in Skibbereen. The guards had found her handbag nearby. There was no note, but enough in her bag to indicate her identity. We all travelled together to Cork that night to make the formal identification. Dad and Uncle Dan tried to persuade Mum and me that we didn't need to see her. I agreed, God forgive me, but Mum insisted, so Mum and Dad went in together through the swing doors and I was left outside with Uncle Dan to wait. I could hear their footsteps echoing over the tiled floor, and then there was no other sound but that of the hum of industrial refrigeration and my breath and Uncle Dan's breath. Once again, time proved useless in the face of tragedy as we waited, maybe minutes, maybe hours, for the news that was not new at all. At one stage Uncle Dan suggested that we say a Hail Mary. I did not understand what possible difference it could make to the outcome.

I think my parents died of grief eventually, although it took a few years. Madame Véronique could shed no light on why Laura had killed herself when we contacted her. She maintained that Laura had been an excellent worker and had noticed nothing strange about her. She said we should be proud of such an intelligent and capable young lady. We took solace from that.

I go over and over what I knew of Laura in the final years of her life. Before we went to France, Laura was a brilliant, flighty, flirty girl with a bright future. During that summer of 1973 she began to show signs of change. I was surprised by Madame's commendation of her. Surprised, but somewhat comforted.

The funeral was devastating. Oliver sent us his regrets in a beautifully written card but could not attend. I was mildly angry about that, amid all the other anger and sorrow I felt. I thought it was discourteous to my parents and me, and to Laura's memory. What could be so important that he would stay away?

With the help of the guards, we had managed to stop the broadcast of the photograph, and kept it out of all but one of the newspapers. The funeral was private, and afterwards condolence cards started to arrive slowly, over many months. Suicide was not discussed then, and people didn't know exactly how to sympathize with our loss, so we dealt with it on our own mostly so as not to embarrass our friends. I don't think attitudes to suicide have changed since then. When somebody dies of cancer, the course of the illness is openly charted and the stages of deterioration catalogued afterwards, but with suicide there is no public discussion and nowhere to bring your grief. It is just the dirty little secret of the bereaved family.

I knew that Laura's decline had started before we left France, and I wondered if Oliver held the key to the mystery of Laura's depression. After all, he was the person who knew her most intimately. I even considered that she might have been pregnant when we left her there, but I know Laura and I can't imagine she would have had an abortion, or given up a baby, regardless of the disgrace it might have brought in those times. The only other theory was that she might have been pregnant and miscarried. I floated the notion to Oliver, but he was stricken by the suggestion. It had not occurred to him. I was sorry I suggested it then, because it must have seemed like I was trying to blame him.

Years later, Oliver named a particularly heroic character in one of his story books after Laura. I appreciated that. He only got in touch again sometime in the early eighties to ask delicately if we could host his wedding reception in L'Étoile.

By that time, Dermot had joined me as maître d' while I cheffed. Despite the awkwardness of our first meeting, it turned out that in fact Dermot was very good with people, remembering their names, their birthdays and their favourite tipples. He was also a super organizer and managed to poach the best waiters from all over town. People returned to the restaurant as much for the superb service and attention to detail they received from Dermot and his team as for the food.

The restaurant was housed in a mews building, and I lived comfortably in the flat on the floor above the dining area. I specialized – *naturellement* – in rustic French cuisine, referred to pejoratively as 'peasant food' by one particularly nasty critic, but quite sophisticated for Dublin at the time, and because we had a liquor licence and took late bookings we quickly became popular with the theatrical crowd; a mixed blessing really – they drank like fish and added some glamour to the place, but often couldn't pay the bill or had to be put to bed in the lounge area at closing time. The stories I could tell of backstage antics in Dublin would put gossip columnists out of business, but we pride ourselves on discretion and Dermot drives me mad sometimes because he won't even tell *me* who's sleeping with whom.

I was happy to hear from Oliver after so long and glad to organize his wedding reception. Also, I wanted to show him that I, too, was successful and in a committed relationship, and that I wasn't a freak.

I was surprised by his choice of bride. Alice. She was pretty, I suppose, but Oliver was known for the beauties he dated and Alice just did not measure up to the usual criteria. She was no Laura. Poor Alice. Whatever happened later on, she was very happy that day. Oliver had no family at his wedding reception. I had long suspected that the hints he dropped about his wealthy parents were a cover. I thought he was probably an orphan, and the lack of family at his wedding confirmed it for me.

I haven't seen Oliver for years now, apart from his occasional TV appearances. I don't think he's been in the restaurant for a long time. When he became a successful writer, I was very pleased for him. Not having children of my own, I read only one or two of the books, and I'm aware that I'm not the target market for them, but I could see how special they are. There have been film adaptations with big-name Hollywood stars, so I've seen more than I have read. His name cropped up regularly in the media, and I could never think of him without thinking firstly, with acute embarrassment, of my self-ejection from the closet, and secondly, with acute sorrow, of my beautiful sister Laura.

Now that the truth about Oliver's character has been revealed, I have been forced to consider if somehow Oliver caused Laura's breakdown. It was over a year after our visit to France when she died, but I can't help feeling more certain than ever that something awful happened between Laura and Oliver that summer, something so terrible that she walked into the sea with rocks in her pockets.

19. Véronique

Michael did his best to persuade Laura to leave Chateau d'Aigse with him, but she refused. She was determined to stay in Clochamps to have her secret baby. She used my tragic situation, claiming that she could take a year out to help me and that she could not simply abandon me, the grief-stricken, childless orphan. Her brother was surprised by her sudden devotion to me. He came to ask me if I was sure that Laura could be of assistance.

I did not tell him the truth of Laura's predicament. I needed help though. My hands were still bandaged, and while my neighbours were generous and kind, I was on my own. Michael insisted that he and his friends would take no payment for their work. It was gracious of him. They were truly *sympathique*. He and Laura were good, good people.

I witnessed Oliver's leave-taking of Laura from my bed-room window. I was afraid that she would make herself pathetic, but she took his hand and whispered earnestly into his ear. She surreptitiously pressed his hand to her belly, but he snatched it away, and never once during this encounter did he meet her eyes. He stood at a distance, fidgeting with his wrists. I thought then how cold he was, how insensitive and uncaring, and I wondered how my father and my son could have loved him. As he followed the others into the truck that was to take him to the city,

Laura began to weep and Michael, knowing nothing of the baby, must have thought her tears were marking the end of her affair with Oliver. He hugged her quickly and gave her his handkerchief. I could see he was trying to persuade her to change her mind about staying, but she was shaking her head. They hugged again, and he got on the truck, and it drove away. She waved as it motored up to the gates, and when it was out of sight she looked towards the spot on the horizon where it had been, and then she looked down and said some silent words to her belly. Even within my grief, I felt sympathy for the girl.

I got to know Laura then. Without the other English speakers around, her French improved rapidly. She was a brave and determined young lady. By the time the others left, she was in her third month of pregnancy, barely showing, but she was more settled now that she had made a plan. When the baby was born the following March, she would give it up for adoption at the Sacred Heart convent in Bordeaux and then return home and go back to her normal life. She had been educated by Sacred Heart nuns in Ireland and trusted they would be kind. I very much doubted that she had any idea what a mother might feel for her newborn baby, but, like I say, I was too preoccupied with trying to inhale and exhale to put much thought into it.

Laura was enormously helpful to me, although it took me time to realize it. At first, it irked me that she would insist on saying prayers for me and with me, lighting candles and blessing herself as she passed the ruin of the east wing. As if any God would allow a child and a war hero to burn to death, but gradually I began to see that there was some comfort in the ritual and that it kept the darkness at bay. Laura's faith assured her that there was a purpose, a reason, and that, while it may never be revealed to us, it was for the ultimate good of mankind. To this day, I cannot say that I subscribe to such a theory.

Laura asked permission to move into the house as the residential workers were mostly gone by November and the bunk-houses were not suitable for the winter. My rule about the house being only for family made no sense now that there was no family. Over the winter months we slowly became friends and confidantes, Laura and I, as she nursed me, fed me, cared for me. How shocked she was when I told her about Jean-Luc's paternity, and utterly aghast that my father had encouraged it. She had assumed I was a widow, and insisted that being a single mother would never be acceptable in Ireland, that in her country it was a shameful thing. It was the same in France, I told her, only I had an exceptional father. She insisted that it was not too late for me to fall in love, to marry, to have other children. I was just thirty-nine then, twice her age, but I was sure that I did not want love. It was not worth the risk of losing it. She nodded sagely, but did not dare to compare her loss of Oliver to my loss, although I knew that was what she was thinking. After just a month, she no longer spoke of Oliver. He did not reply to her letters or take her phone calls. She accepted that it was not possible to make somebody love you and, knowing that, she just got on with her life and with nurturing the one inside her.

I think that towards the end of the pregnancy, Laura was beginning to think of taking the baby home and risking the opprobrium of her family. She used me as an example of how one could lead a perfectly normal life. She was sure that her parents would be horrified at first, but that they would not ultimately turn her away. Her family were wealthy enough to support her, and even if they would not support her, there was an aunt who lived in a remote part of the country where she might live as a 'widow'. I encouraged this, believing that in most circumstances a mother and child ought never to be separated, and encouraged her to write to her family to tell them the truth. She insisted she would wait until the baby was born before making her final decision to bring her child home.

I was very disappointed when I realized that Laura had lied to me and to Oliver. I can understand why she lied to Oliver, of course I can, but there was no reason not to tell me the truth. Even after the evidence was staring us in the face, she persisted with the lie, and I think living that lie ultimately unhinged her mind. Oliver's refusal to meet her eye when he left, and indeed his distancing himself from her, began to make sense when the truth of the baby's conception became clear.

Laura went into labour in the second week of March, a little early, but safely so. Anne-Marie was back by then. We did not call for the doctor. There was no need. Anne-Marie, as well as being our family's retainer, was an excellent midwife. She had no qualifications as such, but she had delivered me, Jean-Luc and half the village. She was always the first person called when waters broke. A quick examination in her bedroom, and Anne-Marie correctly predicted that the labour would be no more than four hours and that, given Laura's health and age, it would not be difficult.

I paced outside as Anne-Marie and Laura laboured together, and then I heard a cry, first Anne-Marie's cry of shock and then, within a moment, the baby's cry. I entered the room as Anne-Marie handed the bundle to a red-faced Laura, but smothered my own cry of surprise when I saw the baby. Anne-Marie left the room with her hands in the air and a shrug. The baby was unambiguously *métisse*, mixed race. She was a beautiful child, with Laura's clear blue eyes, but the undeniably dark curls and facial features of an ethnic African infant. Laura had obviously been unfaithful to Oliver with one of the South African boys. I was shocked. This child was an enormous surprise.

Laura's reaction to the birth was extraordinary. She did not appear to notice at first the baby's colouring, just clasped the child to her, holding on, as if to life.

Once again, I did not know what to say to her. She is black, I said finally, and at first she did not realize what I was saying. Then she looked into the baby's face and suddenly sat up, held the child out from her and stared. She said I was wrong. I told her she must have known this was possible. I gently asked her who the father was. 'Oliver,' she insisted over and over again, until I realized that she must have convinced herself that it was true.

My relationship with Laura changed then. I admit that I tried to keep my distance from the child. I was still raw from losing my own child and was afraid to get close. Laura must have known I did not believe her, and while I did not care if she slept with a black man or a green one, it annoyed me that she continued to pretend. She suggested that the baby's colour might fade after a few days . . . a week . . . two weeks . . . and that her true Caucasian nature would appear soon. Did she really think I could be fooled? That the baby's facial features could change? As I suspected, she bonded with the baby, who she named Nora after her mother, but every day she played the charade of waiting for the dark skin to fade, directing earnest prayers to the Lord Almighty to speed the process. I decided to ignore the race issue, but wondered if Laura might be losing her mind. I was concerned about her.

After some weeks, I gently suggested that it might be time for her to make contact with her family and go home. Laura was extremely anxious now, more than before; bringing a child home to Ireland as an unmarried mother may have been brave, but bringing a black child home would cause a major scandal. France was fairly multicultural even back in 1974 because of the colonies, although more so in the bigger cities, but from what I could gather there was virtually no ethnic immigration into Ireland in those days. I suggested that a mixed-race child might be isolated growing up in Ireland. Again, she insisted that Nora was not mixed race and, exasperated, I let it go.

Another two months passed, and Laura had made no decision; it seemed as if she was actually waiting for the baby to turn white. Eventually, I had to ask her to leave. It may seem cold of me, but I had my own issues of grief to deal with and, to be honest, having a beautiful child in the house again unnerved me. I was jealous and bitter. I gave her the address of the Sacred Heart convent in Bordeaux and found a social worker who might deal with her case. Laura became more desperate and even suggested that I could adopt her baby and that she could come back every summer to visit. I was adamant that this was out of the question and angry with her for being so insensitive, and our friendship cooled significantly.

Nevertheless, I was sad to see her go in the end and she wept a little as I drove us to the station with little Nora in her arms. At the station I kissed them both and wished her well, but even then I was not certain what she would do. I asked her to keep in touch and let me know where she was, and promised that I would never reveal her circumstances to anybody. That was the last I heard of her until I received the devastating letter from her brother Michael before Christmas that same year.

Laura was dead, and clearly it was a suicide. It was obvious from the letter that the family knew nothing of the baby. Michael wrote to me looking for answers, wondering if Laura had been acting strangely, if I knew of any particular trauma that might have happened to her, whether I knew of any reason why she might have wanted to take her life. Among his many tortured theories, he speculated whether Laura could have been pregnant and miscarried.

I gave my reply much consideration, and thought that maybe the family had a right to the truth, but what good would it have done them? I had learned from my friend in Bordeaux that the baby had been handed over for adoption, but Laura had not kept in touch in the intervening months. Even if Laura's family knew, even if they wanted the child, it would have been too late. I wrote a letter telling some truth but withholding the bigger truth: I was shocked to hear the news; I knew nothing of a miscarriage; Laura was a wonderful person who was deeply missed by all at Chateau d'Aigse; she was a fantastic help to me personally in getting over my own loss. I told them to be proud of such a brave and beautiful girl. I sent my condolences to the family and passed on my best wishes to Oliver too.

My father visited me in a dream the night I posted the letter. In the dream, we both knew he was dead and yet it was peaceful and natural for us to be chatting as we used to. He told me to start again and not to allow the past to destroy my future. I must begin to live once more, and not permit the tragedies of the previous fifteen months to blight my chance of happiness. He touched my cheek the way he did when I was a child and kissed the top of my head twice, one kiss from him and one from Jean-Luc.

To try to rebuild Chateau d'Aigse or to sell up and move away? There seemed no way for me to start again on my own. The vineyard, the orchard, the olive grove had not been tended since the fire, but I had neither the inclination nor the energy. The money and the kindness of our neighbours could not be relied on indefinitely either. They felt they owed a debt to my father, but that generation was ageing now and the younger ones owed us nothing, although I knew I would not be refused help if I asked for it.

I eventually decided to sell up, and planned to move to a town my cousin lived in, perhaps forty kilometres from Clochamps, but the day after the estate agent posted the notice in the paper, I had a visitor.

I had not seen Pierre since the week that Jean-Luc was conceived. I had made myself forget about him as best I could. Up until now, he had kept his word and stayed away, but news had filtered through to him in Limoges from his uncle that a minor scandal had followed roughly nine months after Pierre's visit. His uncle had warned him to stay away and not to get involved for fear of disgracing his own family. They knew that I had raised this child with my father until the fire killed Papa and my boy, and that now I was on my own. Pierre and his uncle guessed he must be Jean-Luc's father, and Pierre very much regretted that he'd had no part in his life. He had sought a divorce from his wife, who, he was sure, was having an affair with a local magistrate and had left him, taking their twin girls with her. He had never stopped thinking of me, had written several times over the years and then torn up the letters, still loved me with all his heart, he said, and that I was his first love.

I was astonished that a long-held fantasy could come true, and when this sweet and gentle man offered to care for me, and adore me, I could not resist because love and care were the things I now craved, and to get them from the man who I had not dared to think about for seven years was the answer to a dream. He was shocked and disturbed when I admitted I had chosen him as a father, and wept bitter tears that he never got to meet his son, and what could I do but apologize for my deceit. Gradually, as I related the stories and anecdotes from the brief life of our son, I began to heal and Pierre got a sense of who his boy had been. I assured Pierre that Jean-Luc was as beautiful as his daddy.

This time, with nothing to prove and nothing to lose, I allowed Pierre into my life as I could share my grief and return his love, and we have grown older and closer to the point that he is now my life. We were not blessed with another child of our own – it was too late for me – but I have a wonderful relationship with Pierre's two girls, who come every summer now and bring their own children and help with the cookery school.

Pierre and I married quickly. We reasoned we had spent enough time apart. We decided to take the chateau off the market. Pierre had learned well from his butcher uncle in those early years, and now owned a thriving meat-processing plant in Limoges, which he was able to relocate to our little village, bringing the life and employment to our region that Chateau d'Aigse could no longer provide. We sold the vineyard, the orchard and the olive grove, keeping ten acres of our own, with the proviso that it would remain zoned as agricultural and would not be developed.

We had begun the restoration of the east wing, but my heart was not in it. For me, it was filled with ghosts and unhappy memories. I wondered if there was wisdom in rebuilding this part of the chateau. Who would live in the bedrooms, and who was there to read in the library? It had been destroyed once by Nazis and again by fire, and I could not be enthusiastic about this project. Once the debris had been cleared and the main staircase rebuilt, I decided to shut off the east wing indefinitely. It was not a question of money, though we certainly could not be extravagant, but Pierre convinced me that we were a team and that when the time was right, we would know what to do.

The Irish boy Michael and I kept up a sporadic correspondence after my initial response to the news of Laura's death. He told me he had opened a restaurant, which surprised me – not that he wasn't instinctively good at cooking, but I thought that he'd been interested in hairdressing.

He credited me for introducing him to new tastes and culinary experiences, and insisted that he would never have taken such an interest in food were it not for having such an excellent teacher. He would write sometimes from exotic locations, describing the new recipes or ingredients he had discovered, and I would suggest ways to alter or improve upon them. He invited me and my new husband several times to come and stay in Dublin and visit his restaurant but I never did. The truth is that we would inevitably talk about Laura, and I was afraid that I would not be able to keep up the pretence that she had left Chateau d'Aigse in a happy and healthy state of mind. I allowed the correspondence to lapse eventually. It seemed there was little point in maintaining it.

Michael inspired my project, however. I knew about food, the sourcing, preparation, cooking and presenting of it, and I knew I had taught him well. I began to form a plan, and when I asked Pierre's advice, he caught my excitement and together we consulted architects and drew up a business plan.

Instead of restoring the east wing, we would create a purpose-built residential cookery school with lodgings above. We were insistent that the new building would be architecturally sympathetic to the original house and that it could be built within the existing walls so as not to destroy the aesthetic. It made complete sense. With a little help, I was already entirely capable of feeding groups of thirty twice a day on a daily basis. How much easier would it be if the thirty were to do the cooking themselves? Actually, we soon realized that we could take groups of no more than fifteen at a time as it was not possible to house and instruct any more than this. Structurally, the interior would be very different from the original building and naturally fireproofed from top to bottom.

We have built the business since we opened our doors in 1978, and though I still supervise every aspect, we employ a full-time staff of at least seven, depending on the demand, and I can take a back seat when I want to. We now have an international reputation for excellence, several awards, and visitors from all over the world. I even re-established contact with Michael to spread the word of our venture to Ireland, and he has sent us many new students. Pierre and I have travelled and studied several languages. Fifteen years ago, Pierre sold the meat plant and joined me in Cuisine de Campagne. We use our ten acres to grow fruit, herbs and vegetables, and source our meat and cheeses locally. We have good years and bad years, but there is usually a waiting list for the school. It is only because we opened it that we have finally discovered something else that happened in the summer of 1973, a long-kept secret of theft, deceit and cruel betrayal. Oliver Ryan is a monster.

20. Oliver

About four months after my father's death in 2001, I received a letter from Philip. My brother. His mother had told him of our fraternal relationship and he regretted not knowing of it earlier. He wanted to meet. I deliberated for days over whether to do so or not. What could he have to offer me? How could we possibly have anything to say to each other? Curiosity, however, got the better of me and we arranged to meet privately in a city-centre hotel.

He was extremely nervous. I was not. In appearance, he is not like my father at all. His blond hair is receding. He has not aged as well as I have. In fact, I look younger than he does.

When I arrived, he was seated in a winged armchair in a discreet corner of the lobby. He stood awkwardly and we shook hands. He had ordered sandwiches and a pot of tea. He proffered a cup and saucer. I declined and knew my refusal made him uncomfortable. To be obtuse, I asked the waiter to bring me a large Jameson before I sat to join Philip.

'It's good to finally meet you properly,' he began. 'I haven't seen you since the funeral ... I didn't know then ...'

I was direct. 'What did you know?'

'He told me you were a distant cousin. Mum told me the truth afterwards.'

A cousin. Interesting.

'Did he ever mention my mother?' I couldn't help wanting to know.

'He said . . .' Philip hesitated, 'he said she was a woman of ill repute.'

He said it apologetically and it sounded ridiculous, such an old-fashioned term; biblical, one might say.

'Mum thought she might have been a nurse,' he continued. 'She never knew. He didn't talk about it. Ever.'

A nurse? It was certainly more plausible than Father Daniel's version of events.

'An Irish nurse?'

'I suppose so. I really don't know. They were different times. I am so sorry. So sorry that he abandoned you like that.'

I interrupted him. I can't bear sentimentality.

'You are a priest?' I wanted to know why.

'Yes, indeed, I always, well, I guess, I always wanted to be a priest. Since I was about fourteen years old.'

'To be like him?' I sneered. 'Or to get away from him?'

He looked confused.

'You did know he was a priest? Before . . . me?'

'Yes, yes, I knew that, but I did not want "to get away from him"!'

'You didn't want to get away from a cold and callous bastard like him?'

I could feel my temper flaring a little.

'He wasn't like that at all,' said my brother. 'He was a wonderful father, caring and generous and affectionate. He loved us.'

It was at this point that the waiter delivered my Jameson.

177

The timing was good because I needed to compose myself. My father, *affectionate? Caring?* I had assumed that he treated his wife and his son in a similarly pitiless manner to the way he had treated me. I had expected that Philip had been raised in an atmosphere of dread and that Judith had feared her husband.

I drained my Jameson and ordered another.

'I'm sorry,' said Philip. He apologized for his happy childhood. He fumbled inside the breast pocket of his jacket and handed me an envelope.

'You should have had this,' he said.

My fingers started to twitch. Finally, a letter. Something to explain everything. Perhaps an apology? Perhaps the truth about my mother? There was nothing written on the front. I was embarrassed by my trembling hands as I took it.

I tore it open and saw that it contained a cheque signed by Philip. I didn't even register the amount.

'We should have shared everything,' Philip stammered. 'But I'd like to . . . I'd like . . . if it's not too late . . .'

I shoved the cheque back into its envelope and gave it back to him. I was shocked by my own anger. I wanted to hurt something, to bite something. If I thought my hopes of my father's forgiveness had been buried with his corpse, I was mistaken. I felt suddenly anchorless, weightless, like something very dangerous might happen. Heat rushed to my face. I felt rejected all over again. I was cheated. Why him? Why Philip and not me? Philip's open, honest, innocent face seemed to invite a punch.

'In his entire life, he never gave me anything beyond what he was legally obliged to provide.' I tried to keep my voice low and calm. '*I* made my life a success. Me. Alone. I don't need money. What makes you think your bastard brother needs your guilt money now?' I stood up.

'Please, please sit down, I'm not giving it to you because you *need* it, don't you see? It's not charity; you should have had it before. It is rightfully yours.'

My mind slipped away to thoughts of the lengths I had gone to out of poverty and desperation all those years ago. An awful and dreadful deed that I would not have even considered if I'd had my father's financial support at the time.

'It's too late.'

'I'm so sorry, I didn't mean to be crass. It was just a gesture really. I wanted you to see that I am willing to share anything. My mother wants it too.'

'Your mother knew he abandoned me, and she did nothing about it.'

He had no reply to that, but, dogged, he tried another tack.

'I know we can't make up for . . . what happened, but we could try . . . I could help you . . . to move on? We don't have to be strangers any more. My mother wants us to be friends. You're my brother, for God's sake!'

I could see how anxious he was, how rattled he was. How naïve of him, to think that a chat and a cheque over a cup of tea could fix anything. What kind of fantasy world did he live in? I knew it wouldn't take much to push perfect Philip over the edge.

'For *God's* sake? Really, Philip? You think your God would allow something like this to happen? There is no God.'

179

I had found his Achilles heel. I had questioned his God.

'What's wrong with you?!' he cried. 'I'm just trying to do the right thing here. If I'd known years ago . . . I was told you were bad news!'

'You never questioned it, you never wondered? About "your cousin"?'

'Why would I? I had no reason! I still have no idea why he hated you–' Philip stopped himself, but it was too late and the words could not be unspoken. I walked away. Philip never tried to contact me again. I bet he's glad now that we did not establish a fraternal bond. After all, he was told I was bad news. He was told the truth. Ask my wife.

21. Moya

Con started talking about retiring. He was only sixty-two. Nothing scared me more. At least when he was working full time, I could pretty much do what I wanted, go where I wanted and carry on little liaisons here and there without much need for explanation. The thought of Con's bland, empty face mooning around me 24/7 gave me the heebie-jeebies.

My long affair with Oliver was fast losing its gloss. I'm not stupid. He was turning down more invitations than he was accepting. He didn't even bother to come up with an excuse, just gave me a curt 'no'. I fretted for months, booked myself in for a bit of lipo around the stomach and upper thighs. That seemed to rejuvenate our relations temporarily, but by October of last year I was pretty fed up with being ignored or dismissed and taken for granted, and I plotted a way for us to get time by ourselves. The answer seemed to lie in a two-week residential gourmet cuisine school in the French countryside. Not for us, obviously. For Alice. It changed all our lives. Mostly for the worse.

Dermot from L'Étoile Bleue put the idea in my head. I was dining with some actor friends there one evening, and when he graciously presented the bill, a flyer for this French cooking school was attached. An idea began to form. I suggested to Alice that she would really enjoy it.

She was immediately enthusiastic about the idea, but didn't like the thought of travelling on her own. Con, who must have been hovering somewhere while this discussion was going on, decided for the first time in his life to buy me a decent birthday present: a two-week residential gourmet cuisine course in France. With Alice. He is such a gobshite.

Oliver didn't seem terribly interested when I told him the bare bones of my plan and how it had backfired. He was increasingly distant with me and insisted it would be good for us, Alice and me, to go. I'm not sure how I let him talk me into it. He actually wanted me to be friends with his wife. The few times I had made a disparaging comment about her had been met with a frosty silence on his part, so I kept my thoughts to myself. He said he really did need time on his own to work on his next book. This book, he said, was going to be the most important thing he had ever written. Initially, I was suspicious. Wasn't this the excuse he gave Alice when we were due an assignation? Was he seeing somebody else? He was certainly interested in getting us both out of the way, and showed no interest in where we were going or what we were doing. If I had been Alice, I'd have just taken the credit card and gone on a spree, but God love her, she was never the brightest.

We travelled to Cuisine de Campagne, an hour from Bordeaux airport. I did the driving (even when she drove on our side of the road, Alice was a terrible driver. Oliver refused to buy her a decent car, as she had accumulated so many scrapes, dings and insurance claims that it was a wonder she was still on the road).

The cookery school was based in a small village. The

classes took place in some large modern chalet buildings overshadowed by what must have been a very impressive chateau at one time. One of the wings of the chateau functioned as our lodgings, individual bedrooms opening on to a gallery, below which was a large lounge and communal eating area. Overseen by the elderly but sprightly Madame Véronique, we spent a wonderful two weeks immersed in the culture of French food and wine, with day trips to local bakeries, olive groves and vineyards. The grounds were beautiful. Apparently all the surrounding land had belonged to the chateau until recent years, and we had permission from the local farmers to wander as we pleased. We met other food lovers from Europe, the US and Canada, mostly women our own age, but of course there was inevitably the one handsome single man: Javier, early fifties, handsome, slightly portly. His hair was silver, not that dirty grey you see on Irishmen. Actually silver. He owned a riverboat on the Garonne and was talking of converting it into a floating restaurant.

I admit that the competition from the other ladies was stiff and that I did suffer a tinge of guilt when I thought of Oliver (and none at all when I thought of Con), but Javier was divine. I was very tactical in my approach, at first paying far too much attention to a balding fat Texan and his wife, but then gradually inserting myself into his eye-line as subtly as possible. I am an actress, you see, so I know how to attract attention. I know how to accentuate my attributes. Botox only gets you so far.

In the beginning, I did my best to be discreet. It was very exciting, creeping around the stairwells in the middle of the night. Javier is, without a doubt, the most considerate lover I have ever had. I worried about trying to keep my emotions out of what was, after all, a holiday romance. Charming, sophisticated, but unfortunately stony broke, supported by a brother who was a car dealer, he made me laugh a great deal and promised to get all my films on DVD. Well, both of them. In total we only spent six nights together, but for the first time in my life I felt like I could be honest with this man. I had nothing to lose. Maybe because it was a 'fling', I felt less inhibited. He found me to be outrageous and funny. I have never thought of myself as either of those things. On our last night together, Javier asked me to stay with him. In France! I laughed at the notion. Leaving my husband at this age seemed a bit ridiculous, and the more I thought about it, the more I became convinced that he was always going to be the one who got away, although the idea of a new life, a second chance, was certainly liberating.

Alice was off doing her own thing, mostly hanging out with Madame and the staff, improving her French. I'm sure Alice knew about Javier and me, but she never commented. I imagine that she wouldn't even like to think about it. She had heard me moaning about Con for the last twenty years, but always said that it would all be OK and that we were a great couple. Poor Alice, she only ever saw the good in people. Even her husband.

On that last morning of the second week, I was sneaking through the lounge when I found Alice sitting up. It was about 7.30 a.m.; dawn was breaking over the valley. She didn't seem in the least bit surprised to see me. She asked me straight out, 'How well do you know my husband, Moya?'

I was taken aback. What had prompted this? Had there been a confessional phone call earlier in the evening? Was Oliver leaving her? I had to play this very carefully.

'Jesus, Alice, what are you talking about? Did you overdo it on the wine?'

She looked at me. Stared at me, actually.

'Do you think he's honest?'

'For God's sake, Alice, I think you need more sleep!' I said jovially, trying to keep the nervousness out of my voice. What was I to think? If she had discovered our affair, was that a good thing? Would she leave him now? Should I admit it? After my time with Javier, did I still feel the same way about Oliver?

Alice rose and went to her room silently without looking back at me, and shut the door firmly behind her.

I flew to my own room and immediately rang Oliver. He was groggy, and extremely irritated when I explained in urgent whispers what Alice had said.

'Don't be ridiculous, Moya. She only knows if you told her. *I've* always been careful. What in God's name have you said to her?'

Of course I asserted my innocence, but Oliver was furious.

'I don't need this! I'm writing. I can't have any distractions. Do not call me again.'

I didn't call Oliver again. That day I acted as normal, up to a point. Alice was very quiet. Javier and I spent the morning together saying our intimate goodbyes. I became tearful at the thought of not seeing him again. His eyes darkened with sorrow.

Alice and I left for the airport and spent an uncomfortable

two hours in the departure lounge. I spent all of that time going over things in my head. What did she know? How did she find out *here*? Had she always known? Was Oliver worth it? What did I actually want? And, oh yes, will Con's facial expression change when he hears?

As the flight was called, I knew that I was headed towards a life of dissatisfaction, frustration and boredom.

There was an enormous fuss at the airport when I declared my intention not to board the plane. The bags all had to be unloaded while mine were identified and the flight was delayed. I hugged Alice and apologized. I didn't say for what, but I meant it sincerely. She could work it out for herself.

Javier was just leaving when I returned to the *école*. He beamed from ear to ear.

'*Ma fille*,' he said.

It has worked out well for me. We will live a very different life from the one I always thought I wanted. Javier and I plan to run our little River Bistro together. He will do most of the cooking and I'll do the front-of-house stuff plus a spot of cabaret thrown in for free, depending on the clientele. We hope to make enough during the summer to live comfortably in a small villa through the short winter months. My children were hurt and furious but will just about forgive me, I think. Kate and her boyfriend are coming to visit next weekend, and when they see how happy I am, they will understand. Con will be a sweetheart about everything financial. Kate tells me that he seems relieved that I am gone and has taken to wearing a kaftan around the house.

I am horrified by what Oliver did to Alice. You think you know someone. It turns out that I rang the house on the very night of the assault. I am in a state of shock, to be honest.

I know I wasn't fair to Alice. Life wasn't fair to Alice. But mostly, Oliver wasn't fair to Alice. So far, the few people that knew about our affair have kept their mouths shut, but when the trial begins next month, the muck raking will begin in earnest. I have a new life now and the last thing I need is for the sordid details of my past with Oliver to jeopardize my future with Javier.

I could make a fortune if I sold my story, but I won't. Out of respect for poor Alice.

22. Véronique

Towards the end of October last year, two ladies from Ireland arrived at Cuisine de Campagne, both in their late fifties. I noticed them immediately because they seemed such unlikely friends. One of them was loud, wore too much make-up and blatantly set out on a mission to seduce the only available single man in the group. The other was quiet, bookish and less inclined to socialize. I felt sorry for her as it soon became obvious that her friend had decided to abandon her for the duration of the holiday. I introduced myself to Alice and invited her to join us on several evenings, and together with Pierre, we ended up discussing all the things one is not supposed to: politics, religion, race, and so on. Her friend Moya had made the booking online, so it was only on the last night that I noticed Alice's surname as she signed the guestbook.

'Ryan?' I said. 'The first Ryan I ever met was an Irish boy working here the summer of 1973. His name was also Ryan, Oliver Ryan.'

'But that's my husband's name!'

We laughed at the coincidence. She was astonished, and we quickly made the connection that she was the same Oliver's wife when she showed me some photos. He was older but still handsome, and there was no mistaking him. We spoke for most of the night. I was happy to hear that he was a successful writer. I recalled that Michael may have mentioned that in correspondence. Alice was shocked when I recounted the pivotal events of that season, of the fire and the death of my son and my father. She knew that Oliver had spent summers abroad – she actually fell in love with him on a foreign trip to the Greek islands – but it seemed that he had never told her much about the summer of 1973 except that he worked on a vineyard. I thought this odd because, whatever his trauma at the time, it was bizarre to me that all these years later he had never mentioned the fire or the deaths. The story of that summer is something one could not easily forget, particularly Oliver. With regard for his privacy, I did not tell Alice of the bond Oliver had with Papa and Jean-Luc, realizing that if Oliver had not talked about it in nearly forty years, he had buried it for a reason. I was discreet as ever, and did not mention Laura except as one of the gang, although it seemed that Alice had heard of her. Alice and Oliver had had their wedding reception in Michael's restaurant, although apparently Michael and Oliver were no longer friends, and she mentioned that Michael's sister had died tragically young. Poor Laura.

'Oliver was an enormous help to me after the fire. He was very upset.'

'Oh, that's lovely to hear – I mean, that he was helpful,' Alice said, proudly.

'Yes, of course he was sad about Papa and Jean-Luc, but he insisted on clearing out the library where he and Papa had worked together. They tell me he did the work of ten men in the week after the fire. He must also have been devastated because all of the work he had done with Papa's stories went up in smoke. He worked so hard transcribing them for my father.'

'Your father wrote stories?' Alice said.

'Yes, I am a little surprised that he never told you any of this. My father secretly engaged Oliver to transcribe all the stories he had written for Jean-Luc.'

'Children's stories? Well, perhaps that's where he got his inspiration. Oliver writes books for children too. How lovely that it was your father who must have given him the idea. What were your father's stories about?' she asked.

'I can scarcely remember, it was so long ago, but the central character was Prince Felix, and there was a trusted servant called Frown, an evil witch and a flying chair.'

Alice narrowed her eyes and clutched her hand to her breast.

'Prince *Sparkle*,' she said, 'and *Grimace*.'

I didn't understand. 'Are you feeling all right?' I asked.

'Tell me more about the stories,' she said, and her voice had grown thin and shrill. I did not know in what way I could have offended her.

When I could not recall the details specifically, Alice became agitated.

'Are you sure your father wrote the stories, that it was not Oliver?'

It was my turn to be offended by her insistence.

'But what a preposterous question! My father began to write these stories when he was released from prison after the Liberation, long before we met Oliver!'

Alice sprang up from her chair and started pacing. To my astonishment, she began to describe the stories I had not heard in many decades.

'There is a young prince who lives in a land of sunlight and joy. An evil queen and her army come from the gloom to invade and occupy their land. She banishes the sun and orders them to live in the darkness, or to die. The Prince's servant invents a magic chair that flies beyond the stars, and every morning Prince Sparkle and his servant Grimace would fly far behind the moon until they found the sunlight. They would capture the sunlight in their cloaks and smuggle it back to their kingdom and share it with their people.'

It was my turn to be shocked.

'How . . . how could you *know*?' I asked.

'Oliver wrote it. I illustrated it!' she said. 'I have illustrated all the stories!' and she broke into sobs.

My shock turned to anger, and I suddenly felt the need to defend my long-dead father from her insinuation. 'Papa enjoyed writing them,' I insisted on explaining. 'He read them to me as a child. It was part of our bedtime ritual, though he wrote less when I grew older. But as soon as I became pregnant with Jean-Luc, he began writing them again with renewed vigour and he continued writing these stories until his death, despite the physical discomfort it caused him.'

'How did he write them? Have you no copies?' Alice demanded to know.

'They were written on loose sheets of paper all over the house. Papa had primarily employed Oliver to transcribe them into leather-bound books so that they could be compiled in just a few volumes.'

'Why did he ask Oliver? Why Oliver?'

'I don't know. He liked him. Papa treated Oliver like a son. My father did not like to type anything himself. But he insisted that the stories should be made of ink.'

191

To my horror, Alice began to relate more of Papa's stories to me. The names of the characters and the places were different – Papa's witch was now an evil queen – but the stories were undeniably the same.

Truth can cause more pain than lies, I think. Some secrets are best left as secrets. The facts are simple. Oliver stole Papa's stories. I had no way of proving it. The stories existed solely in Oliver's typed notes. The only people who remembered their original versions were long dead.

Oliver used a pseudonym to write these books: Vincent Dax. How clever and sinister. Having no children, I never bought one of his books. Pierre's girls were not readers. When I looked him up on the Internet, I realized what an industry had been built around Prince Felix, or Prince Sparkle as he was in Oliver's version. Films, stage musicals, merchandise. Oliver has made millions from my dead father and betrayed his honour.

The revelations certainly upset his wife. We talked through the night until almost dawn. It seems that Papa's stories were what attracted her to Oliver in the first place. He was shrewd with the stories, releasing just one every year or two, and has made them last for all this time, although it seems now that he has run out, as he has published nothing for five years. We worked out that he had spent almost twenty-five years carefully translating and plagiarizing my father's work. Alice insisted that he was currently working on a book but that he was finding this one particularly difficult. It was to be his first adult novel, but he claimed to be suffering from writer's block.

It seemed that Oliver was not even a good husband to Alice. She was aware that he had been unfaithful. Possibly even with her travelling companion, Moya. He was dismissive of her work and of her opinions. He was intolerant of her friends. He could not get on with her mentally challenged brother, and upset him to the point where the unfortunate man became aggressive and had to be put into a residential care home.

'Why do you stay? Why do you not leave him?'

'He needs me . . . needed me.' She corrected herself. 'He told me that he could not write the stories without me.'

'What about love?'

'I thought that *was* love.'

The next day, Alice and Moya left together. Moya returned alone some hours later. The ridiculous woman was leaving her husband – for our solitary single man, it seemed. Always with the Irish, there is the drama!

Alice emailed me to tell me that she had found the leather-bound books and was going to confront him, but asked for my patience. I never dreamed that he would attack her, but I was keeping abreast of all news of him and when I read later that he had been arrested for her assault, I realized that I must somehow be involved, that the books were the source of the trouble. I contacted the Irish authorities. I supplied the motive for the attack. I am finally going to Ireland, to give evidence at the trial. The lawyers tell me that he will admit to the plagiarism. I am horrified by what he did to Alice, and a part of me wishes I had never met her and that we had never discovered the truth.

The truth remains. Oliver has betrayed us all.

Papa did not write those stories for publication. He

wrote them for me and for my precious little boy. I know it should not matter to me that Oliver made money from them. If I had found the books, I do not think it would have occurred to me to publish them, but they were mine.

What kind of a man is Oliver to have done such a thing? I wonder if he really loved my father at all, if he even cared about my son. Was it an opportunistic moment, when he found the books intact amid the debris and thought he could just take them? Or had he been making secret copies all along, knowing that we would never publish them ourselves? Alice told me that Oliver had no mother to speak of and that he and his father had been long estranged, that in fact she never even met Oliver's father. So could it be that after my father's death, he found the books and thought of them as his inheritance?

I recalled what Oliver said to Laura about her pregnancy, about not wanting *another* child. But then I think of Laura's infidelity and it stops making sense. Perhaps Oliver was trying to make a family out of mine. Who knows? He is just a thief.

Of course, I went into the town the day after Alice left and bought all of the books. The stories are as I remember them, but astonishingly, Alice's illustration of the central character, Prince Sparkle, is uncannily the image of my boy, Jean-Luc.

23. Oliver

The month before I left school, my father sent a cheque for fifty pounds in the post and a curt note suggesting that I find myself a flat and a job as I was soon to be eighteen and could not expect to be supported any further.

I had no idea what I was going to do with my life, but Father Daniel took me aside and counselled that my grades were good enough for university and that I could always come back to the school to teach when I had my degree. He came to my rescue once more and offered to pay my college fees and found me a bedsit in Rathmines.

It took quite a while to get used to living alone and preparing food for myself. Up till then, my life had been organized with military precision. I had become institutionalized in my years at boarding school. I was not used to being alone. I wrote to my father telling him of my new address, but received no reply. I worked in a fruit market early mornings and weekends to support myself and to keep myself occupied, but college life was enjoyable nonetheless. A lot of students were living away from home and I could pretend to be like everybody else. I was not an outstanding student by any means, although I was top of the class in French. Trying to work and socialize on my meagre earnings meant that study was sometimes neglected, but I managed to earn respectable grades despite that.

Having had a taste of freedom, I knew for sure that

I could not go back to the school, nor had I the temperament for teaching.

By early 1973, I was dating Laura. Wild and beautiful Laura. So different from the other girls. I loved her, I thought. Maybe if we had stayed in Dublin that summer, everything would have turned out differently; maybe we would be married, happily ever after married.

As my second-year exams approached, Laura hatched a plan for us to spend a summer abroad on a working holiday. I thought it was a pipe dream, but Laura wrote to farms and vineyards and canning factories all over Europe looking for jobs and eventually got a response from a farm in Aquitaine. We were invited to an estate in a tiny town called Clochamps. There was a chateau and a vineyard, an olive grove and an orchard. It sounded ideal. Mindful of my previous summers in captivity, I was eager to travel, expand my horizons and see what the world had to offer, and also to spend time with Laura. The plan, of course, was somewhat derailed by Laura's parents, who, although fond of me, did not approve of the two of us going off together by ourselves. However, there was nobody more determined than Laura, who persuaded her brother Michael and five others to join us. Chaperones, in the eyes of her parents. It was to be paid work with accommodation included, and thankfully, Father Daniel agreed to lend me the fare to get there.

I loved it from the moment I arrived. I was used to manual labour from my extracurricular job in the market, and while the others took a little while to adjust, I found it relatively easy. Irish summers could be grey, damp and miserable, but here the sun shone every day and although we could see marvellous lightning storms at night at the other end of our valley, the rain did not fall in Clochamps. My college mates complained of heat and sunburn, but I easily acclimatized. The meals provided gratis were simple but excellent, wine was free too, and Laura and I easily found time and space to be intimate away from her brother and the others.

The elderly owner of Chateau d'Aigse befriended me early on. I translated for the others. My spoken and written French were good, and he was genuinely interested in me and wanted to know what I was studying, how I intended to use my degree, my plans for the future. After two weeks, Monsieur asked if I would be interested in doing some transcribing work for him. I readily agreed, thinking that the office work would involve typing invoices or some kind of record keeping. That is what he led his daughter to believe. He asked for my discretion and overpaid me. He introduced me to his grandson, Jean-Luc, the most beautiful and charming child I will ever know.

On the first day I reported for duty in the library, Jean-Luc was there also and Monsieur asked me to take a seat while he read his grandson a story. I was intrigued. Jean-Luc formally stepped forward and shook my hand. I knelt down to his eye level and returned his greeting with a little bow. He laughed and looked up at his grandfather and, pointing at me, he called me 'Frown'.

As Monsieur began to tell the story, I watched the boy's face as he perched on his papi's knee. He was transfixed by the tale of a happy young prince of a fantastical land and would exclaim in the middle of the telling, would hide his eyes at the arrival of the bad witch, and clap his hands in excitement at our hero's escape in the end. I realized that Frown was a character who protected the Prince, and that the Prince was clearly modelled on Jean-Luc. I, too, thought the story was wonderful and said so to Monsieur d'Aigse. He was very happy to be complimented and explained that he had written a series of these stories on and off over the last decades, but that they consisted of handwritten notes. He wasn't even sure how many stories there were. He had developed a palsy in his right hand and could no longer trust his own penmanship. My task, he said, was to type up all these stories to be pasted into some expensive leather-bound books he had bought for the purpose. It was to be our secret. He thought his daughter would disapprove that I was not being used for estate work, but I think she very quickly guessed what I had been employed to do. She did not interfere, however.

As I heard his stories, I thought they were good enough to send to a publisher, but Monsieur insisted that they were written solely for his family and that when Jean-Luc was older, he could decide what to do with them.

Laura began to complain bitterly that I was not spending enough time with her. She was right. I was enjoying myself with my two companions, and on several occasions I was invited to dine with the family. Madame Véronique was a little more distant than her father and son, but I loved being there with them and was reluctant to leave when the working day was done.

I tried to humour Laura, promising that I would devote the next night to her, but I rarely kept those promises. The old man treated me like a son. He thought I was a good man. A family was more seductive than anything she could offer me, although I continued to sleep with her because, after all, a man has needs.

As I set about typing these stories and then laboriously pasting them into the leather-bound books, I found myself growing closer to the old man and the little boy. I was included in their secret world, and they accepted me without question. I could not get enough of their company, and it suddenly seemed to me as if I had somehow been wasting my time with Laura, as if no mere romantic relationship could be worth more than this platonic one between three menfolk who might, in some realm of possibility, have been three generations of the same family. I lost almost total interest in her affection and her vibrancy, and by now used her only for sex. All of the things in which I had previously delighted were now meaningless, as if the spell of the enchantress were broken. This new connection felt somehow purer.

For the first time in my life, I felt able to confide my private thoughts. I told Monsieur of my father's lack of interest in me. He was clearly appalled and he shook his head in wonder, as if to say, 'How could a man not be proud of this boy?' and I loved him for it. He suggested that there was enough transcribing work to keep me busy for more than one summer, and I agreed enthusiastically to return the following year.

The truth is that I did not want to leave. There wasn't that much time left. The idea of returning to my drab and lonely bedsit filled me with revulsion, and even thoughts of Laura's affection failed to quell my growing anxiety about the future.

At this time, I was worried about my prospects. I did not have the family support that most of my fellow students had, and my existence in Dublin was hand to mouth. I hid it well, bought good second-hand clothing, borrowed books, stole stationery, and when in private survived on tea, bread and whatever fruit I could scrounge from the market. I let my friends think my parents lived in the countryside somewhere, and never allowed any visitors to my bedsit. I stayed in their homes and met their families and got more insight into how the other half lived. I desperately wanted what they had, but there seemed to be no way for me to achieve it. I was jealous of their lifestyle and their lack of anxiety about what lay ahead. I was headed for the lowest rung of the civil service, without the all-important contacts that everybody else seemed to have, or the financial backing to set them up in business. When I borrowed the fare to France, Father Daniel very gently informed me that he could not continue to fund my life beyond college. We were both mortified. I was grateful for everything he had done for me. He again suggested that I could come back to the school and teach, but that was now out of the question. I had finally escaped boarding school and there was no way I was going back. I was getting plenty of female attention, but I foresaw that when it came to marrying time, no family of good standing would allow their daughter to hitch herself to a penniless nobody. I needed a plan.

What could I do to force the d'Aigses to invite me to stay here with them? How could I endear myself to Monsieur d'Aigse to the extent that he would 'adopt' me? I probably could have seduced Madame Véronique if I'd put my mind to it, but I was not attracted to her, and regardless, my dream future entailed my being accepted as me, without pretence. I did not want to live a lie. Not then.

My French was good enough to be able to converse with the locals. I knew of Monsieur's several acts of bravery during the war. He was a hero in the commune. Could I be a hero too? What if I were to save a life? I began to fantasize about how I could achieve Monsieur's iconic status. It amused me in my idle hours to imagine being embraced as one of their own. What if I could save Jean-Luc's life? Wouldn't that earn their loyalty and gratitude? Wouldn't they beg me to stay and live with them for ever, as part of the family, their protector? But I reasoned I could never save Jean-Luc's life without jeopardizing it, and that, obviously, was out of the question. Still, I could not shake off my romanticized dreams of the future. It became as real to me as if it had already happened, and I regarded the old man and his grandson with ever growing affection.

Then, I thought, what if I were to save the chateau? Surely that would be on a par with saving a life. And maybe it was something I could engineer if I put my mind to it. The idea came together slowly over several weeks – though in the beginning I believe I thought of it as comforting fantasy rather than a plan; something to puzzle over, as if teasing out a mathematical equation. But gradually I began to look around with a sense of purpose. I scrutinized the chateau in a new way.

It struck me that fire was something I understood. Any boy who spent time in a boarding school was well versed in the art of pyrotechnics. It is said that necessity is the mother of invention, but often it is in fact boredom. We knew what burned fastest, loudest and most colourfully. We knew what caused explosions, what made a damp squib, how to cover up the smell of sulphur. I knew how to start a fire, and I also knew how to contain it.

The harvest started in early September so all hands were required in the vineyard, but by then I knew my way around the ground floor of the house and I knew that the most flammable part of it must be Monsieur's library, with its dusty collection of books, maps and ancient ledgers detailing the commerce of the house over centuries. If I could be the first on the scene, if I could save the house, then I would be the hero. I could be employed to restore the library to its former glory. I was the only person who knew where everything in it was kept. Surely, Monsieur would see the wisdom of keeping me on? He would blame himself: a spark from his pipe must have escaped unnoticed, he would think, and smouldered slowly until it caught fire.

Shaking Laura off that night was the difficult part. She had something to tell me, she said; she needed time alone with me. I assumed she was going to tell me that her brother was a queer, but everyone knew that already. I put her off, saying that I was exhausted and needed to sleep. She insisted it was urgent; she had to tell me something important. I lost my temper with her then, told her I'd had enough of her clinginess, her jealousy of my work in the house, her demanding my attention constantly. I told her our relationship was over and that she should find somebody else to follow like a dog. I was unnecessarily cruel. I regret it. I was too absorbed by my own skulduggery to give much thought to her feelings.

Monsieur and Jean-Luc came down to the vineyard to say goodnight to me that night. We were working till dusk, and I had not been inside the chateau for a week.

'Goodnight, Frown!' said the little boy, and laughed, delighted with himself.

'Good night, Prince Felix!' I responded.

I must have drunk six cups of coffee that night to keep myself awake. I was exhausted, naturally, but exhilarated by the task I had determined to undertake. Nobody stayed up too late, aware of another arduous day ahead. I lay in my bunk, listening to their breathing, waiting for each room-mate to succumb to hard-earned slumber. Michael tried to engage me in whispered conversation about Laura. He had noticed she had seemed upset earlier in the evening. I admitted we had had a row, but avoided the details of my vindictiveness. I assured him that I would talk to her in the morning and that we would patch things up. He was content with this, and soon he was breathing evenly.

As soon as everyone was asleep, I made my way silently up to the back door beside the lean-to building and into the library. The leather-bound books and handwritten papers that I had been working on were kept on a shelf in a corner of the room by the door. It struck me that these must be saved from the fire. How grateful might they be to discover that the summer's work had been rescued and that Jean-Luc's most personal inheritance was intact?

I put them to one side while I amassed a bundle of loose typing paper all around the bookcase and doused it with lighter fuel. I planned to be the one to discover the fire in about twenty minutes so that I could be the hero who stopped the fire going out of control. I lit the touch-paper and watched for a moment. I hoped the fire would catch in time. Hiding the leather-bound books near the bunk-house, I crept back to wait for the appropriate moment to sound the alarm.

I checked my watch about every six seconds, but time seemed to relax its grip and the minute hand of my watch appeared to freeze. I held it to my ear, and *tick, tick, tick*, yes, it was working as it should. Minutes before my planned alarm-raising, I heard my name being called softly from the door of the bunk-house. Damn, Laura. I got up and went to her and we had the same argument again that we had had earlier in the evening, but this time she began to fight back.

'You can't just dump me with no explanation! You can't just leave me! We love each other!'

She was raising her voice, growing hysterical, and I knew I must get away from her, go up to the house and put out the fire. Others had emerged to see what the fuss was about, and Laura was by now grabbing at my shoulders, wailing at me, 'Why? Why? What have I done?'

I tried to get her to shut up. 'Nothing, you've done nothing, I just can't . . . I don't . . .'

I was aware of shadows moving around us. We had woken everyone. Michael emerged out of the gloom. He was clearly annoyed and I think embarrassed that Laura was making such a spectacle of us. He took control and ordered us both sternly to go back to bed. What was I to do? Maybe thirty minutes had now passed, but no sign or smell of smoke or fire had yet reached our quarters, and I thought perhaps it might have gone out. I reluctantly followed him back to the bunk-house as Laura was led away weeping by one of the girls. I lay down, furious, as Michael began to give me a whispered lecture about Laura's delicate 'feelings'. Should I just feign storming off in a temper, so that I could go and check on the fire? How much longer could I wait? Could the fire have blown itself out? Michael was still going on and on, but suddenly he stopped. 'What's that smell?' he said, and he leapt out of bed and ran to the door.

Michael was the one to raise the alarm. He could have been the hero, not me. But we were both too late to save lives.

I did not know about the paraffin cans in the lean-to shed, behind the door. I had never been upstairs in the house, and somehow I got the impression that there were no bedrooms in the east wing. I never meant harm to the boy or his papi, but I am solely responsible for their deaths. I will never forget the sound of Madame Véronique's screams. It has haunted me for nearly forty years.

I was just about putting one foot in front of the other in the days that followed, going through the motions of empathy and sympathy, but I felt nothing at all, just a needle-sharp aching wound in the core of my soul. I tried not to sleep, because waking to the horror of the truth every day was unbearable.

Sweet Laura tried to comfort me. It was known that I had grown close to the dead, but I could not take her platitudes and rejected her all over again. I worked with everybody else, trying to clear the mess and the destruction and trying to avoid contact with Madame Véronique, whose family I had murdered.

I cleared out the library, but there was nothing left of it except some maps and an ivory paperweight that were kept in a metal box. Madame came to me and specifically asked about the leather-bound books, among other things. Monsieur must have told her about our project. I told her they too had been destroyed. Then I broke down and wept, and she held me in her bandaged arms and I felt worse. The fire service concluded that a stray ember from Monsieur's pipe, which somehow ignited the paraffin in the lean-to, must have sparked the fire.

Four days before we were to leave, Laura told me she was pregnant with my baby. I could hardly ingest the information and ignored it and her, but she was everywhere I turned over the following days. In my grief I snapped at her finally, insisting there was no way I could have a family. My child had just been buried. She stared at me, and I realized what I'd said and realized I'd meant it. She cried and pleaded, but I was not going to concede any more emotion. I was already spent. I told her to get herself fixed up and to send me the bill. Somehow, I would scrape the money together to pay for it. She cried more.

Laura wisely decided not to come home with us. I assumed she'd find a little doctor somewhere who could sort her out. Michael was baffled by his sister's insistence on staying on at Chateau d'Aigse, and negotiated between Laura and her parents in expensive phone calls that went on for two days. I presented it to him as philanthropy on Laura's part. She simply wanted to stay and help Madame Véronique, and sure, what harm could it do. He knew by then that we had split up, but clearly she had not confided any of the details in him. I could not look at her or Madame

Véronique on our day of departure. My shame would have been too obvious.

My shame was not so great, however, that I did not have the leather-bound books containing every story ever written by Vincent d'Aigse wrapped in a towel at the bottom of my suitcase. I'm not sure why I took them. Maybe I wanted some part of my two friends to take with me. Their innocence and their purity. Maybe I needed a reminder of my guilt. I had deliberately lied to Madame Véronique, but these stories were all I had left of those two precious souls and I could not relinquish them.

Back in Dublin, in my sunless bedsit, I spent a week in bed, not leaving the house or speaking to anybody. How could I even begin to explain that I only meant to be a hero, and not a murderer?

The books were on the dresser accusing me, and yet I could not bring myself to dispose of them. I did not look at them or open them. Finally, I dragged myself out of my decline. I left the house and went to a second-hand furniture shop where I bought an old wooden box with a sturdy lock. I came home and locked the books into the box and hoped that I would forget where I had hidden the key.

Laura was not so easy to forget about. She wrote several letters, trying to convince me that 'we' could keep the baby, that her parents would stand by us eventually. For a while, I considered it, but ultimately dismissed the notion. Marrying into a wealthy family was not a bad option, but raising a child? When I had just killed one? I do, after all, have a sense of morality. Then she wrote to say that she was going to have the baby in France and that I must go and join her there to raise our child. Another two months went by, and she wrote that she had changed her mind and was going to keep the baby anyway and bring it home, regardless of my involvement, sending me into paroxysms of panic. I never replied to any of the letters, but waited with increasing anxiety for news of the baby's birth.

The due date came and went and I heard nothing. But three months later, I assume in a last-ditch attempt to make me change my mind, she sent me a pink plastic hospital bracelet with 'Bébé Condell' written on it. There was no letter attached, and I was relieved that my name had not been used. Apparently, I had a child, a baby girl.

An unwanted child had an unwanted child. Perhaps the apple did not fall far from the tree after all. There are several clichés I could use to illustrate the fact that I am undoubtedly my father's son. Like him, I did not want a baby. Maybe what I did was worse, by not acknowledging the child at all, but Laura was a sensible person and I knew that if Michael wasn't allowed out of the closet, then Laura knew how difficult it would be to bring home what was then termed a 'bastard' child.

In August 1974, I heard that Laura was coming home. Nobody mentioned a baby. I assumed she had placed it for adoption. I hoped the baby would have a family that loved her. But at the back of my mind, I had a doubt that there had ever been a baby. I wondered about the possibility that Laura was never pregnant in the first place. I thought she may even have had an abortion or may have miscarried it. Why did she send me the bracelet, and not a photograph? If she was really trying to convince me to keep it, wouldn't she have sent me a photograph? Also, my instincts told me that Laura simply would not have given up her baby. She was braver than me.

I saw Laura in college the following October and avoided contact. She was thin and sickly-looking and appeared not to socialize. It was rumoured that she was suffering from depression. Michael came to me and asked if I would talk to her. I could not refuse. I approached her one day in the library. She was standing in front of a book-shelf in the anthropology section. I greeted her and asked if she would like to come and have a coffee with me. She did not speak, but took my hand and placed it on her almost concave belly, just for a moment, and then she walked away. It was the same gesture she had made when I left her in France.

I was angry with her and wrote her a coded letter then, reassuring her that she had done the right thing but insist-ing she should just get over the past and get on with her life. She did not reply to my letter, but returned it. I found it in shreds, posted through the slats of my locker.

The girl was clearly unstable. Within a month or two, I heard that she dropped out of college, and then Michael rang me to say that she was dead.

I tried to have a reaction to this. I tried to cry. I expected guilt or anger but instead there was a strange emptiness, another void to add to the one already at the core of my soul, if such a thing exists. I had rejected her and hurt her, but I felt nothing, except that she was one less reminder of that summer. I am sorry that she did not think life was worth living. Another man could have loved her the way she needed. She was very beautiful, after all, and adorable, pleasant, easy company most of the time, before France.

Several men I knew would have wanted nothing more than a date with the alluring and elusive Laura Condell. I regretted that she died but it was not my fault. None of this was my fault. I was supposed to be wailing and gnashing my teeth apparently, but I had really *done* guilt by then, and it was of no benefit whatsoever.

I left college the following year with a 2:2, a good enough degree. I would have liked to start my own business importing wine or something like that, but with no capital and no collateral, it was out of the question.

Out of financial desperation and seeking guidance, I even went to my father's house one evening and rang the doorbell. I stepped back and waited, saw the curtain twitch, saw him seeing me, and then the curtains were drawn by an unseen hand and the door remained shut.

Eventually I got a dull job working alongside unambitious people in the offices of the Inland Revenue as a clerical assistant, the lowest form of life, but it allowed me to rent a flat on Raglan Road, a better part of Dublin. It didn't take too long to move house. One battered suitcase and a refuse sack containing my mugs, pots, kettle and radio. And the locked wooden box, its key in my pocket.

My new home was even smaller than the one I had before, but location, location, location. I lived on beans and eggs and tea, and met up with some of the old crowd every summer to go travelling, having scrimped since the previous year. I lied about what I was doing, pretended to be rising through the ranks of the diplomatic corps. My sense of envy festered.

By early 1982, I was getting rather depressed. It had

taken me seven years to move up one grade from clerical assistant to clerical officer, and that was only because someone died. I was sick of the penury, sick of the pretence and sick of myself. It seemed that I was doomed to this misery for the foreseeable future. There was no one to rescue me. Unable to control my thoughts, I recalled the hero who could have rescued me, if I hadn't killed him. I remembered that kind old man, the boy, and a time when there were possibilities, when I was surrounded by decency. The box on top of the wardrobe in my room underneath its layer of dust called to me.

Several times in the intervening years, I had been on the point of throwing out the leather-bound books, thinking that doing so would ease my guilt. But I never did. It would have been sacrilegious. They represented something beautiful, something that I had destroyed, but which nevertheless I needed. I could not explain the need, not then. On that night, in that moment of torment, I only wanted to remember.

With shaking hands, I unlocked the box. I read the stories again. There were twenty-two of them in total, some already neatly typed up by me in the pages of the leather-bound books, some written in blotted ink by a shaky hand on loose sheets that I'd carefully placed between the pages. I did not sleep for a week thereafter, but then a few bottles of cheap wine helped me to forget the child for whom they were written and the hand that wrote the original drafts. Remembering had been a mistake. Or so I thought.

Gradually, it dawned on me that these stories could be my escape route. If they had not died, if I had become somehow part of their family, would these stories not also have become mine? I was the only one that the old man had trusted to transcribe them. Why? Why a strange Irish boy he did not know? Why not a local scholar? Why did he choose me? If Jean-Luc was no longer around to benefit from these stories, well then, why not me? The fire was just the result of a minor deception that went awry, I told myself, desperate to justify my plagiarism, and once I had made the decision, it was easy. I only needed to rewrite them in English, change any identifiable details and publish them under a pseudonym, just to be sure. If I were to publish a couple of thousand copies in an Irish print run, I might be able to secure a future for myself.

The first publisher I approached expressed interest, and that expression of interest allowed me to engage an agent who quickly negotiated a rather quick and unprecedentedly lucrative deal on the strength of the fact that I could pitch at least ten sequels on the spot. I immediately bought a good linen suit and a sports car on hire purchase from the proceeds of the advance.

A month later, I met Alice, who was to be my illustrator, at the launch of another book whose author my agent also represented. I could not believe my eyes when I saw her first drawings of Prince Felix. Without any guidance, she had captured the essence of a small French boy, nine years dead.

I invited Alice to come away with a small group of us to Paros on holidays. I planned my seduction terribly well and it was surprisingly easy, made easier by the clown that was Barney, who not only permitted his girlfriend to come travelling with me, but also arranged with her mother to look after Eugene in Alice's absence. It wouldn't have made a difference in the end. She was predisposed to love me because, as she later confessed, she was in awe of my stories.

By the time the first one was published, I already believed that I'd written it. The advance blurb was so positive that I immediately thought my father might change his attitude towards me if I was successful, if he had something to be proud of, so I invited him to the launch. He did not come. I made no further attempt to contact him after that.

Alice and I got married and I lived happyishly ever after. Alice was happy enough too, I suppose, once she'd resigned herself to being childless and got used to the idea of the imbecile being in a home, although my liaisons upset her from time to time, when I was careless enough to be caught, usually when Alice had done something to irritate me. But I was never careless with my darkest secret and kept it locked away in its wooden box.

It turned out that my meek and mild-mannered wife was more sly and devious than I could have imagined. Three months ago, she returned from her little cookery trip without Moya. Moya had finally got the courage to leave her husband for a Frenchman she'd met at the school. I had long ago come to the conclusion that Moya was a pain in the arse and had been in the process of dropping her, though God knows she did not take the hint easily. Now that Moya had left Con for another man that wasn't me, I felt nothing but relief, though admittedly my pride was a little wounded.

I noticed that Alice was particularly quiet, and Moya's early-morning phone call from France a few days previously had put me on edge. With nothing to lose, had Moya spitefully told Alice of our affair? When Alice had caught me out before, it usually led to weeping and stony silences for days and recriminations and stomping off to the spare room for a month until I promised to give up the floozie and never do it again. But I knew that this one would hurt more deeply. Alice had always thought of Moya as a friend, and it had been going on for years, not just one of my ten-weekers. When I broached the subject of Moya with her, she only said how devastated Con must be and that she hoped Moya would find happiness, but Alice's mood was odd. She had a sudden confidence that I didn't quite trust. I thought maybe she knew about my affair with Moya but was relieved that Moya was now out of the picture. I rationalized that either Moya's absence made her more secure or she felt finally superior to Moya. I was quite wrong.

Four days after her return, on that chilly November evening, Alice prepared this terrific meal and said nothing at all until the raspberry roulade.

'Did you get the recipe for this on the cooking trip?' I said, trying to be breezy.

'It's funny that you should mention that. I had a very interesting time. You never asked exactly where we went. Let me show you the brochure.'

I saw the word 'Clochamps' before I saw the picture of the chateau and was instantly shocked into speechlessness.

'Madame Véronique remembers you very well.'

I still could not say anything. She stood up, took the fork out of my hand and lowered her face to mine.

'You are a fraud, a liar and a thief!'

So I punched her. It seemed like the most natural thing in the world.

The really ironic thing is that by the time Alice discovered my true deceit, I was actually working on my own book. The first truly authored by me. It wasn't a children's book at all. It was a very dark tale about neglect, abandonment, grief and lost children. It was loosely based on the story of Cain and Abel. I wonder where I got the idea?

My God, writing is boring. Starting was the worst part, and it has taken me almost five years to write sixty pages. All I had been doing for the previous twenty-four years was reading, parsing, translating, and then using my trusty thesaurus to change the words around to take the Frenchness out of them. That was hard work too and took a great deal of skill. Though, as it turns out, writing does not come naturally to me. Under the guise of Vincent Dax, I regularly gave interviews to the media, exclaiming that the *Prince of Solarand* books pretty much wrote themselves. It was my little insider joke. Now that I have attempted to write, I can understand why other authors were so infuriated by my statement. Well, I continue to be baffled by theirs.

'I was born to write!' they might say, or 'I couldn't do anything else!' Pathetic.

If anybody had bothered to work it out, I did credit the old man with writing the books, in the form of my pen name.

My wife, I had always thought, was a mouse, but now

she had sharpened claws and revealed a feline arrogance I had never seen before. When I returned after my quick diversion to Nash's, I found she had broken the lock on the wooden box, and the leather-bound books were on the kitchen table beside her. Her suitcase, only recently unpacked from her trip to the French cookery school, stood beside her. So she was leaving me. Fine. No problem. Off you go.

Only then, she calmly told me that the suitcase was packed for me, that she was returning the books to Madame Véronique, that I must leave *her* house. I told her she was being ridiculous. It did not have to be this way. I started to explain myself. Where was the harm in publishing what would probably have been discarded anyway?

Alice did not want to listen. My whole life was a lie, she said, reminding me that it was the books that had made her fall for me in the first place, reminding me of some of the more cringe-worthy things I may have said to her at one time or other – 'I couldn't write these without you', 'You're my inspiration' – and of the many dedications to her on the acknowledgement pages: '. . . and finally my best to Alice, without whom none of this would be possible'.

I realized something I had failed to notice for the last thirty years. You don't have to love a person. You can love the idea of a person. You can idealize them and turn them into the person you need. Alice loved the person that she thought I was. One way or another, I have managed to kill all the people who have loved me so far.

Where is my mother? Where is she? Couldn't she have loved me? I may have killed her too. The whore.

Jean-Luc, my little friend, I remember the small arc of your arms around my shoulders and the heft of you as I piggybacked you around the terrace.

Monsieur d'Aigse, who showed me nothing but generosity and kindness, you opened your heart and your home to me and made me welcome when I offered you nothing in return but death, and then later, theft.

Laura, you were a normal happy girl until I chased you and somehow poisoned you to the point when death was your only option.

Shame flooded my head and I felt again like the boy who was not good enough to see his father because he had spilled juice on himself, like the boy whose father inspected him like one would a horse, looking for defects.

When I attacked Alice for the second time, these thoughts went through my head as I punched and kicked and bit and slammed and dropped and wrenched and tore.

24. Barney

I couldn't believe my eyes when I answered the door very late that night three months ago to find Oliver covered in blood. At first I thought he'd been in a car accident. He was shaking like a leaf, but he said he wasn't hurt and when I looked a bit closer, I could see that he didn't have any wounds.

'Jesus, what happened!?' says I.

'It's Alice,' he says, 'she needs help.'

I'm glad my mam is dead now because if she'd been around for this, her nerves would have been shot and I wouldn't be allowed out of the house.

I left Oliver sitting in a chair in my hallway and ran over to Alice's. The hall door was wide open and I went in, dreading what I was going to find.

She was in the kitchen. At first sight I thought it was just a load of laundry piled up against the back door, waiting to go into the machine, but then I noticed smears of blood across the floor and on the wall above and I realized that it was Alice. God, the image of that will never leave my head, so help me. I knelt down by her side and lifted her head. Her breathing was shallow, but she was conscious. I was crying now, as I tried to hold her and reach the phone on the wall behind her. Little frothy bubbles of blood were coming out of her mouth. I roared at the 999 people to get an ambulance and gave them the address. They said they'd send the guards too, but I dropped the phone because I couldn't hold Alice and talk to them at the same time. I wanted to be talking to her. In films on the telly, they always say that you should try and keep the victim awake because if they lose consciousness, they die, so I was talking to her, telling her to hang on, and she was looking at me, the beautiful eyes that I had loved my whole life, even though I had no right. She was trying to say something but I told her to save her energy, and the sight of the blood pouring out of her was terrible and I held her close and said, 'It won't be long now, hang on, love, hang on.' She did say a word and I guessed it before she finished saying it. 'Eugene,' she said and then she passed out.

The ambulance came and took her away, and then the guards arrived and I remembered that Oliver must still be sitting in my hall. I might not be the sharpest tool in the shed, but by now I obviously knew he'd done it. I remembered how snotty he'd been in Nash's earlier in the evening when he threw a pack of fags at me. He was covered in *her* blood. So I told the guards where to find him, and watched as they escorted him out of my house. He looked up at me, all that swagger and confidence gone out of him, and I realized that no matter how educated he was, how rich or how posh, I was a better man than him. I always had been.

All those years ago, when he stole her from me, I didn't put up a fight. I practically gave him my permission. I thought Alice deserved someone better than me. I should have fought for her.

I visited her in the hospital the next day but she never regained consciousness, so now I visit her once or twice a week and I hold her hand and talk to her because in films sometimes that works and you can get a fella back to normal. I tried bringing in old songs she liked and I put headphones on her head, but she never stirred. One day I was chatting away, reminding her of the time we went to Galway and got drunk on the port, and she opened her eyes and I roared for the doctors, but they said it was nothing and that just because she opened her eyes doesn't mean she'll get back to normal. I saw a film, a foreign one about a fella who was in a coma like her, but he knew what was going on and you could tell because one of his eyes would follow you round the room. Alice opens her eyes now from time to time, but not like she's seeing anything, just as if she's blinking but in reverse, if you know what I mean. She smiles sometimes. I hope she's remembering happy times.

I don't think she's going to get better now, but I still like to go in and chat because you never know.

I started going to see Eugene too. He's just the same mad fella he always was. Delighted to see me. The other day, didn't he lift me up in a chair and off we went! I was scared out of my wits and this bossy one screams at him to put me down, but weren't we only having a bit of a laugh.

Oliver has signed over guardianship of Eugene to me. It was all done through solicitors. It was complicated because Alice is his next of kin, but she's not dead and Oliver's her next of kin even though he half killed her. Oliver had the nerve to ask if I'd go and visit him. Apparently, he wants to 'explain' himself. Fuck him.

Enough of him. I'm having Eugene come and live with me. There's social workers and assessments and all sorts involved, but I'm pretty sure it's going to happen. I've cleared out Mam's room, and I've wallpapered it, and I've bought loads of books for him. Not *those* books, obviously, but other ones. I got a CD player too for his room. The fella tried to sell me an MP3 player, but sure what would I want with one of those. I already had to buy all my records on CD after the record player broke and I couldn't get a replacement. It'll be the MP3 this week and something else next week. I can't keep up. I got a new car too. The back seats are high up so that Eugene will be able to see out properly. I'm giving up smoking. It's really hard, but it wouldn't be right with himself in the house. Eugene and me will have a grand time.

Every time I visit him, he asks when Alice is coming. I can't tell him yet. I'll take my time and think of something. Maybe he won't be upset to visit her in the state she's in. I don't know, but I know when he moves in with me, he's going to want to run around to his old house and see her. It's all boarded up now. I'll have to think of something to tell him.

The papers called it 'The House of Horror'. It seems to me that if you stub your toe at home these days, they call it 'The House of Horror'. They are having a field day. In the first month afterwards, I had to go in and out my back door because of what they call the 'media scrum'. They want my story. My story is that I loved and lost. They won't get many headlines out of that.

Epilogue
Oliver – Today

Infamy is a lot more interesting than fame, it seems. It is not just the tabloids who think so. An acre of newsprint was used up in documenting the fall from grace of the successful writer who turned out to be a plagiarist and a wife beater. Pundits who might previously have described themselves as close personal friends are now granting interviews in which they claim that they always knew there was something strange about me. They speculate that I was in the habit of beating my wife, despite the lack of evidence at the trial to support the theory, and they relate conversations that never happened that imply I was always violent and that Alice was terrified of me.

One rag published a school essay from over forty years ago to highlight my bad prose and to illustrate my unfocused narrative. The Ph.D. students who once flocked around me like acolytes claim I have destroyed their careers and their credibility. Diddums. Critics claim that somebody who had no children could never have written stories that appealed to them so much. That is not what they said at the time. In fact, they said back then that it was because I did not have the responsibility of children that I hadn't fully grown up and therefore could more easily access the mind of a child. Fools. They have delved into my past and my background and asked questions about my parentage. They found no more dirt than my father's early priesthood.

My brother Philip wrote to me six months after the trial. I can only imagine his sanctimonious hand-wringing. I'm sure he agonized over whether writing to me was the 'right thing to do'. He offered his services as a chaplain or confessor in case I should ever want to 'unburden' myself. He assured me that God's forgiveness is possible and that, if nothing else, he was 'always there to listen'. Bin.

I miss Alice.

I thought I would not be able to eat the food here, but actually it's quite good and there's plenty of it. I have eaten less well in Michelin-starred restaurants, though the presentation could use a little attention.

The building in which I am housed is a decrepit Victorian institution, impressively daunting on the exterior and drab with neglect and stained Formica surfaces on the interior. Men and women are segregated. That suits me fine.

I have my own room, so in a lot of respects it is better than boarding school was, although my housemates are a peculiar bunch of miscreants. I remember years ago, one of my less imaginative colleagues in the civil service had a 'witty' sign on his desk that said, *You don't have to be mad to work here, but it helps!* It wasn't even funny at the time.

It is not a *mad* house, however; it is a sad house. Everyone here has committed crimes deemed to result from their insanity. I feel like I am here under false pretences, but that is nothing new for me. Almost my entire life has been a deception of one kind or another. I am not obliged to mix with the others, and I spend most of my time voluntarily alone.

There is a working farm within the grounds, and even though it has been quite a while since I did any manual labour, I have enjoyed getting my hands dirty. I am no longer a young man, but I am fitter than I have been in decades.

I am a model 'patient'. They don't call us prisoners in the nuthouse. 'It's political correctness gone mad!' I hear all the time. I agree. The guards and nurses are decent, and I cause them no trouble. It is generally acknowledged in here that my crime was a 'one-off'. I 'snapped'. I am on a low-dosage antidepressant and go placidly amid the noise and haste.

I will have a 'mental health review' every six months to decide if I am sane or not, but if I am declared sane, I might be released and that would never do. I have decided to stay here, because even though I am not a danger to society, or myself, I do not want to leave. I plan to fake a suicide attempt if they ever suggest it.

The house has been sold. All proceeds from the sale went towards the continued care of Alice and maintenance payments to Barney Dwyer for Eugene. Alice is in a private facility. The lawyers told me she is in a beautiful room and is receiving the very best of treatment, but she will never know it. It is likely that she will continue in this state for years. Copyright and royalties from the books have been assigned to Madame Véronique and I am denounced internationally, but particularly in France, for stealing from a war hero, and profiting from his death and that of his grandson. If only they knew that it was worse than that, that I was the one to cause their deaths. I have never told the analysts that part of my story. It would cause such a fuss. Why add arson and murder to the list of my crimes?

Journalists have made several attempts to visit, offering to ghostwrite my story. The insult. I turned down their offensive requests. All but one particular French journalist. At least, I assumed she was a journalist. Her letters to me were more formal than the others, and she was not easily put off. Her name is Annalise Papon. I ignored her first five letters and then finally responded to the sixth, thanking her for her interest but declining an interview, regretting that I would not be putting her on my visitors' list. There is nobody on my visitors' list.

A month ago, she wrote back the most startling letter.

She is apparently a lawyer, not a journalist, but she has no interest in my case or the charges against me. She says she has recently become a mother for the first time, and the birth of her precious son has led her on a path of discovery that she almost wishes she never began.

Her birth was registered in the city of Bordeaux, France, as being on the 11th of March 1974 in a small village called Clochamps. Her name at birth was Nora Condell. She was placed for adoption on the 20th of July of the same year. Annalise is hoping that I might be able to help her trace her father. It has been implied to her that her mother named me as her father.

Laura's baby. My child.

She admits that she is confused as to how to feel about this, that after two years of searching records she discovers her father could be a violent criminal and a plagiarist.

Laura's name is on Annalise's original birth certificate as her mother. She knows from her research that Laura is dead and that it was a suicide. She assumes her birth might have precipitated her mother's death. She has been able to track down photographs of Laura through her old school's website, and although the shape and colour of her eyes are similar, in one distinct aspect she is not like Laura at all. She began to do some searching to see if she could find her father instead. The father's name is not listed on her birth certificate, but Annalise has made contact with the adoption social worker who dealt with Laura. Apparently Laura insisted that the father was an Irish student called Oliver Ryan, but she was not allowed to name me on the birth certificate. Annalise was able to quickly discover that Oliver Ryan was better known as the infamous Vincent Dax. She has studied photographs of me from the covers of my books and has seen film footage of me on YouTube from some television appearances, and she has noted a striking resemblance between us in our mannerisms and way of speaking that cannot be ignored; and yet, she says, 'something is wrong' because Annalise is of mixed race and, clearly, 'you and my mother are white Europeans'.

My hands began to shake again, and I laid the letter on to my desk so that I could stop the words from dancing.

My daughter is nothing if not dogged in her pursuit of truth.

I have recently availed myself of a personal genomic service to have my DNA genetically profiled. It seems that my ethnicity is specifically at least 25 per cent sub-Saharan African, which would indicate that one of my parents is of mixed race, i.e. one of my grandparents is black. I was able to find out that both of Laura's parents are Irish born, but can find very little information about your parentage. I note that your colouring is darker than the average Irishman, although your features are undoubtedly 'white'.

Studies in genomic theory are advancing at a rapid rate thanks to the new data available from DNA mapping, and science now tells us that skin colour is not determined by only one gene. Instead, it is determined by many (polygenic inheritance). Therefore there are many factors that have a role in the skin colour of a person besides the skin colours of their parents. It may still be possible that you are my father if you have any ethnic ancestry.

She proposed to visit me in order to do a DNA swab test. She assured me it is a simple, non-invasive procedure. She was coming to Dublin and hoped that I would agree to meet her.

Having watched the video footage of you many times, I think it most likely that we are, in fact, related. I do not know if this will be a source of shame to you or what your views of racial harmony might be, but please bear in mind that when I set out to find my parents, I did not for one moment think that I might find one in jail. The wonderful parents that raised me would be horrified if they thought that this might be the case, and I have no wish to tell them. Nor would I want to go public if this turns out to be true.

I put the letter aside. I left my room and wandered out to the yard. The guard smiled and nodded.

'And how's Oliver today? It's a cold one, eh?'

'Do you have a cigarette?'

'Indeed and I do.'

He handed me a cigarette, solicitously lit it for me and tried to engage in some light banter, but I am known as a loner so he soon stepped away to leave me to my customary solitude.

Father Daniel was right about everything. The story about my father and the native girl was true. What became of her and what was she like? I have an image of her in my mind, dressed in tribal clothing, walking away from her village and her life into an African sunset, thinking herself cursed by my birth. I find myself weeping for her at odd moments and, strangely, missing her, and wondering if she ever missed me. I think of my father and imagine his public humiliation when I was born, caught in his lie of denial, and I feel a small degree of pity for him.

Then I think of Laura, and how confused she must have been by her child. Who would have believed that I was the father? Certainly not me. This is why she could not send me a photograph, and why she could never have brought her baby home, not in those days. How could she have explained her baby's paternity? She must have questioned her own sanity. There was a kind of accepted racism at the time among the Irish middle classes. It went unacknowledged because it never had to be confronted. In Ireland in 1974, I could count on one hand the number of black people I had ever seen. Laura's child would have created a scandal for her family. Also, it was one thing to be an unmarried mother, but another thing altogether to be a *single* unmarried mother with a black child she had no way of explaining. I did that to Laura. I made her think she was insane. I killed her.

My daughter Annalise came to visit me today. She is beautiful like her mother and, I suppose, like *my* mother and, in a strange way, like me. It is some kind of genetic accident that I was born white, but this girl is undoubtedly mine. Mine and Laura's. I still had the slimmest doubts right up until the moment I saw her. She has the same clear blue eyes and the sense of vibrancy and purpose that Laura had when I first met her, but her skin colour comes from my mother, via me.

It was awkward at first, but I used my old charm to put her at her ease until the atmosphere was at least cordial. I made enquiries about her son, *my grandchild*, and she showed me a photograph of a small boy, perhaps two years old, sitting in between her and her husband. He has a mischievous smile on his face and I can tell he is happy. I am glad. I asked her if she was happy, and she grinned quickly and ducked her blue eyes.

She sat opposite me, and I watched as she nervously buttoned and unbuttoned the cuffs of her expensive silk blouse, and I did not want to deny the truth to myself any longer.

I could, however, deny it to her.

I admitted that I knew Laura well, that we had dated in college and that we had spent a summer together in

Bordeaux. I told Annalise that her mother was brave and beautiful and would have desperately wanted to keep her. I denied knowing that Laura was ever pregnant, and could not explain why she might have named me as the father. I said that there were some South African workers at the vineyard in the summer of 1973 and implied that Laura must have had a liaison with one of them. I recalled them as good, strong and cheerful boys but regretted I could not remember their names.

I told her that there would be no point in doing a DNA test. I told her all about my parents, Mary (née Murphy) and Francis Ryan, a priest at the time of my birth. I suspect Annalise must already have known of this detail. I even recalled for her my earliest memory: I am sitting on my father's knee in a large garden while my laughing parents embrace each other on a bench. We are the only people in my world. My mother has red hair; she wears spectacles and lipstick. My smiling father is in a high-waisted suit. The bench is under a tree. One of the boughs of the tree hangs low and heavy with blossoms over my father's head. My mother carries me over and puts me into a swing. There is a safety bar across it. She pushes me gently, and I laugh because I like the feeling of the air rushing through my stomach. I want her to push me a little higher, but she is afraid to do so. My father takes over the pushing and she goes back to the bench to sit down. My father pushes me higher and I am thrilled. After a little while, I use my feet as brakes. I feel the gravel and note a cloud of dust rising. I run over to my mum and jump into her lap. She hugs me close to her, and I know that my father is watching with pride. I am warm and safe.

I told Annalise about how my mother left us some years later, and how my father remarried a woman who did not want to raise me. I feigned upset. I said I didn't like to talk about it. Annalise was sympathetic and did not press for details. I explained about how I was raised in a boarding school.

'I'm afraid there is no mystery, and that you have had a wasted journey.'

I wished her luck with her continued search.

She seemed relieved, I think. Happy to know that, after all, her father was not the monster who sat before her. We shook hands. Her hand was warm in mine.

I have destroyed enough lives. She is better off not knowing. This, finally, is a secret I am proud of keeping. Protecting her is an act of unselfish generosity. I try to be good.

Acknowledgements

Heartfelt thanks to:

Marianne Gunn O'Connor, my agent, who deserves her excellent reputation for incredible support, and Vicky Satlow, for her determination on my behalf. Patricia Deevy, my editor, for gently helping me to shape my story as you now see it. Also, Michael McLoughlin, Cliona Lewis, Patricia McVeigh, Brian Walker and all of the team at Penguin Ireland. Keith Taylor, Lisa Simmonds and Holly Kate Donmall at Penguin UK, and copy-editor Caroline Pretty, for painstaking editing, proofing and production work. Alison Groom and Lesley Hodgson, for suitably sinister jacket design.

Sincere gratitude for expert research advice from:

Mark Shriver Ph.D., Professor of Anthropology and Genetics at Pennsylvania State University; David MacHugh Ph.D., Associate Professor of Genomics at University College Dublin; and Kieran Gaffney, Charge Care Officer (retired) at the Central Mental Hospital.

Personal thanks to:

Alison Walsh and Clodagh Lynam, for excellent advice, and Kevin Reynolds, Clíodhna Ní Anlúain, Lorelei Harris, Jesper Bergmann and Cathryn Brennan, for broadcasting my early scribblings.

All of my beloved friends and family members, including in-laws, who were forced to read this multiple times. And especially to my dad, who passed on to me his love of literature.

My husband, Richard, for everything. I adore you. x